SMALL FAMILY WITH ROOSTER

SMALL FAMILY

WITH ROOSTER

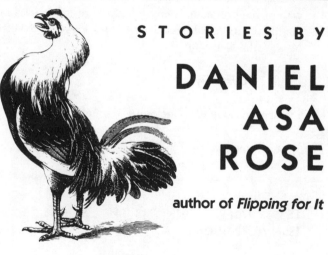

STORIES BY
DANIEL
ASA
ROSE

author of *Flipping for It*

ST. MARTIN'S PRESS · NEW YORK

Design by Debby Jay

Library of Congress Cataloging-in-Publication Data

Rose, Daniel Asa.
    Small family with rooster.

    I. Title.
PS3568.07616S6   1988   813'.54   88-1923
ISBN 0-312-01826-6

First Edition

10 9 8 7 6 5 4 3 2 1

For my Parents

CONTENTS

CONTENTS

PART II

Now I have my answer! Again at last, the answer!
What is the theme to this commotion?
The shock to learn that we are all connected
That we are all growing older
That we are all liars
And that beauty exists.

—Anonymous (Six Dynasties)

PART I

THE ELEPHANT STORY
(THE STROKE, I)

The phone booth in Grand Central was missing its door, and Mr. Deerfelt was forced to do something he didn't want to do: raise his weak voice and shout. "I have misgivings," he shouted.

His daughter was sitting on the bed of her college apartment in Providence, where it was not noisy, but she was shouting, too. "What do you mean, 'misgivings'?" she shouted. "What sort of misgivings?"

"I don't know," Mr. Deerfelt shouted.

"About meeting my boyfriend?"

"Yes!"

Caroline Deerfelt could hear people and carts rushing past her father, also someone singing in a drunken fashion, also what sounded disturbingly like a rocket being launched. She could imagine his large soft body bent over in his doorless telephone booth to concentrate on what she would say next. "Come anyway," Caroline said firmly, standing up and carrying the phone to her desk. "I really want you to come."

Four hours later Mr. Deerfelt was in a large, easygoing cab in Providence. Beside him sat his daughter, looking so happy and excited that Mr. Deerfelt wanted to ride around all night and just watch the white streetlight crossing and recrossing her lovely pure face. But he was worn out from the train, and when they got up the hill to her apartment—it was a very nice quiet garden apartment with a spare bedroom—he could barely keep his eyes open, and he had to say good night.

"Good night, then," said Caroline, throwing her arms around him, "and get a good night's sleep, but in the morning Lucas is coming by, and you're going to think he's terrific. The best!"

"I'm sure I will," said Mr. Deerfelt, and with a smile that had a hint of alarm in it he went into the spare room where there was a bed all ready for him, and, on the nightstand, a dish of crocus flowers that he could smell in his sleep.

Later that night Caroline, a freshman, called Lucas, a senior, from her bedroom. She asked him if he didn't mind too much that her father was there, and Lucas said no, that he understood her father came first.

"I love you for that, for saying that," Caroline whispered into her mouthpiece. "For understanding."

"Caroline," said Lucas, "I understand that he's no longer a musician, and he's no longer a husband. All he is, is a father."

———◇———

The sun was gigantic and colorful in the morning when Lucas rose, and Lucas felt both powerful and light-headed:

encapsulated in protein. He felt great. He put on his bicycle shorts and his sneakers and a great orange parka, and he managed to extract his bicycle from the closet in the television room, where all the bikes were stored. It smelled much better outside than inside the fraternity house, and he rode through chilly spots in the mild spring air, and the college was sleeping, and he was riding on cobblestones. Mad! He was mad about her!

Mr. Deerfelt was also up early with the excitement of seeing Caroline. He padded about, clattering cups and saucers until she awoke, and then the two of them sat at the old three-legged kitchen table with the sun pouring in on the wood, and they laughed, and interrupted each other, and Mr. Deerfelt loved her so much he could hardly keep from hugging himself—his bloodstream seemed enriched from being near her again. Caroline could barely sit still with anticipation. "You're going to love him, Daddy," she kept promising, and she kept jumping up from the table in her exuberance and fetching different things to show her father what her college life was like, mostly things having to do with Lucas. Mr. Deerfelt was still in his baggy gray pajamas, to which he'd affixed a tiny pink crocus, and he weighed what his daughter told him. He fingered a photo of the young man, and he quit laughing, and he quit wanting to hug himself, and after some time there was a silence, which he was expected to break, but he couldn't. Suddenly a look of grief, soft and weightless, touched Caroline's face. "But you still come first!" she cried, grabbing his bad hand and urgently kissing the palm.

Mr. Deerfelt could feel his heart heave at this, his eyes grow moist. Shyly he drew his bad hand back, and cradled it in his good one.

Mr. Deerfelt was the victim of a stroke. Half his body,

5

his entire right side, had been stricken, in his sleep, several years before. Two years of physical therapy at a leading hospital had improved his condition enough for the hospital to feature him in a brochure promoting its services. A smiling Mr. Deerfelt was pictured being assisted down a set of stairs by a smiling nurse; a gallant Mr. Deerfelt was pictured fox-trotting with a large black woman in a gown identical to his. But Mr. Deerfelt no longer looked like the pictures in the brochure. His hair was choppy and he didn't always remember to shave. He had put on weight and, living alone, he spent a good deal of his time in pajamas. The stroke had meant the end of Mr. Deerfelt's career as a musician, and more. He was forced to put away his oboe, and it languished in its case; finally he'd sold it to supplement the welfare checks. He was a huge, soft man with a not-low voice and he had grown used to thinking of himself as ridiculous. He felt he was of no use to anyone and he lumbered around New York thinking that there was one thing glorious in the world—and that was this girl: this warm, nervous, beautiful daughter. The doorbell rang.

Caroline leapt to the door and opened it and the first thing she saw was a great glint of sunlight reflected off the handlebars of Lucas's bicycle, which was propped against a thick budding forsythia in the yard. Then she saw Lucas, and for an instant she didn't know who he was. She swallowed her breath, her face became flushed, and she thought she wanted to close the door.

Lucas yanked her several steps into the yard and Caroline dove her cool hand into his shorts. She closed her eyes and held her breath, and when she squeezed him a minute it was as though she were absorbing the strength and tranquillity she needed. The bare branches above them rocked at different levels in the wind. Then, smiling and clearing their throats, the two young people came inside to the kitchen where Mr. Deerfelt sat in his gray pajamas with his back to them, reading the sugar box.

"Mr. Deerfelt, I'm delighted to meet you," said Lucas, jutting forth his hand. Mr. Deerfelt jumped as if taken by surprise. He twisted in his chair and tottered to his feet and hoisted his arm from the shoulder to meet Lucas' grasp. "Ah, hello, we meet at last," Mr. Deerfelt said with strange courtliness. "Sit down and have some breakfast with us, won't you?" he said. They smiled at each other shyly and intently and then Mr. Deerfelt turned away and succeeded in dropping with perfect aim to his seat. "We have corn bread and date bread and here's some butter and here's some cream cheese," he listed, nudging each item across the table to Lucas, who looked at Caroline, laughing a little. She laughed a little, too.

"He never eats anything for breakfast!" Caroline said, and then Mr. Deerfelt realized what the joke was: that it was funny to offer someone something he didn't want. He felt fat and foolish and he chuckled good-naturedly.

"I always have an early lunch," Lucas explained, and Mr. Deerfelt said, "Ah!" as if a great mystery had been cleared up—and then Mr. Deerfelt closed his eyes and he began to see elephants.

"Goodness!" he said. "More elephants!"

Caroline and Lucas looked at each other. "Elephants?" they said.

Mr. Deerfelt opened his eyes mirthfully. "Yes," he said. "It's very entertaining. Whenever I close my eyes these days, I see at least one or two elephants in my mind's eye; I recall them ambling about."

Caroline and Lucas looked dubious.

"It's very entertaining!" repeated Mr. Deerfelt. "Haven't you ever seen anything in your life, from your travels or

7

your experiences, that you could recall whenever you closed your eyes?"

Caroline tilted her face to the ceiling and closed her eyes. "Oh yeah," she said ardently. "You're right. I can see lots of things."

Mr. Deerfelt settled back in his chair and closed his eyes and smiled a gentle smile.

Lucas waited a moment before clearing his throat. "Are you still recalling them?" he asked.

"Just now," Mr. Deerfelt said, "I'm recalling how majestic one of them was, roaming about in his natural habitat. Oh, he was beautiful! And I'm recalling how pitiful it was to see another one locked in a cage at the zoo." Mr. Deerfelt opened his eyes and thought for a moment. "Well, all zoos aren't that bad, but most of them are!" he said. "Have you ever seen an elephant roaming free in his natural habitat?" he asked Lucas.

"No, sir, I haven't," Lucas said.

"They're majestic creatures!" Mr. Deerfelt assured him.

"Daddy saw them when he used to go touring with the orchestra," Caroline explained, opening her eyes to gaze upon the sight of both men seated around her table. "And Dad," she said, quickly turning to her father, "Lucky here worked on a whaling ship one summer."

"A *scientific* whaling ship," Lucas was quick to add. "We didn't kill them; we tranquilized them and took samples of their blood. Those whales are majestic!" he said.

"What did you call him?" Mr. Deerfelt asked his daughter.

"Lucky," laughed Caroline, blushing a little, but at the same time feeling proud. "All his friends call him that."

"I don't even notice anymore," said Lucas, lowering his eyes but also feeling proud.

Mr. Deerfelt looked disapprovingly at his corn bread,

and he pressed a few crumbs of it into his plate with his thumb.

"That's what they do to elephants," Mr. Deerfelt said sadly. "They shoot them with tranquilizer bullets, and then they ship them to the zoos."

"They shouldn't do that," his daughter said, after a moment.

"They shouldn't," agreed Mr. Deerfelt. "It's pitiful. It's a damn pitiful shame, and I'd like to see it stopped." Absently he put the end of his thumb in his mouth and sucked the corn-bread crumbs off. When he had swallowed them, he shook his head. "They're the real kings of the jungle," he said.

"Well, lions are," corrected his daughter.

"Lions *are*, but lions *shouldn't be*," Mr. Deerfelt said carefully. "Elephants should be. Elephants are ten times more noble and majestic than lions." Mr. Deerfelt thought about that for a moment, fingering the crocus on his pajama lapel. "Perhaps I shouldn't put it that way," he said. "Lions are, also, noble animals. But elephants should definitely be kings."

Lucas went to the refrigerator and poured himself a glass of orange juice and returned with it to the table. "Anyone else want orange juice?" he asked.

"No, thank you," said Mr. Deerfelt, lowering his hand erratically to the table. He was rather shocked that Lucas had helped himself like that. He felt enormously depressed suddenly.

"Tell me, Lucas—"

"Oh, call him Lucky."

"Really?"

"Go on!"

Mr. Deerfelt took a shallow breath through his nose and blinked. "Tell me, Lucky—why is it that you have an early lunch instead of a breakfast? That's not a sensible eating habit, if you ask me."

"I don't really know why," said Lucas, cocking his head to consider. "I guess I don't like breakfast foods. I don't like cereals. I don't like muffins. I *hate* eggs," he said with a smile." "Eggs always look like the raw form of some other food, no matter how they're cooked."

"Even scrambled?" asked Caroline.

"Especially scrambled!" said Lucas.

Caroline visualized a scrambled egg being the raw form of some other food. "Whew," she said, with a look of delight. "If I saw them that way, I wouldn't be able to eat scrambled eggs, either."

"And you'd be missing a very enjoyable food product," Mr. Deerfelt labored to point out.

There was a silence; then Caroline accidentally bumped her foot against the back of Lucas' chair. "Oops, sorry," she said, with a smile.

"Anytime," Lucas said with a smile that mirrored hers.

There was another silence. Mr. Deerfelt shuddered slightly.

"Is anything the matter?" asked Caroline.

"No, no," said Mr. Deerfelt, chuckling a bit and tapping her hand. "I was just wondering what was stopping your friend here from having some corn bread or some date bread."

Lucas turned about in his chair to face Mr. Deerfelt. "I don't know!" he said, with such a pleasant smile, and such a pleasant nodding of his head, that it seemed the issue had been resolved to everyone's satisfaction. Caroline sucked in her breath and nodded her head with exactly the same conclusiveness. Even the motes of dust in the sunlight seemed to dance with conclusiveness. It was a very quiet dance.

Mr. Deerfelt closed his eyes. He smiled sadly and bowed his head to his plate. "I'm just now recalling an elephant," he said, "who had the last three feet of his trunk bit off."

"No!" blurted Caroline and Lucas, with a laugh of surprise. "It's not possible!"

"Yes," said Mr. Deerfelt, with closed eyes. "I'm afraid it *is* possible."

"But how could he eat?" asked Caroline.

"He couldn't eat," said Mr. Deerfelt. "He was starving."

"Then how was he staying alive?" asked Caroline.

"He wasn't staying alive," said Mr. Deerfelt. "He was dying."

Caroline and Lucas raised their eyebrows at each other; then something like a shrug passed between them, and they smiled slightly and stirred, Lucas zipping his parka up and down, Caroline taking his glass and draining the last of his orange juice, then looking up excited—on a private wavelength.

"What about hard-boiled?" she asked.

Lucas looked pleased as he thought about hard-boiled for a minute. "Raw," he said.

"But not as raw as scrambled?" she asked with a smile.

Lucas zipped his parka up and down. "No, not that bad," he said, sharing her smile.

"A lion bit it off," Mr. Deerfelt said.

"*What?*"

"A lion bit it off," he said, with closed eyes. "So that this poor creature could no longer sustain himself. And oh! You should have heard the fuss he made, because the pain must have been quite something."

Caroline made an impatient clicking noise with her tongue. "Oh, who cares," she said.

For an instant the supply of sunlight pouring onto the

wooden table dwindled. Caroline hardly recognized her kitchen without the weight and heat and steady cheer of the sun. She looked around worriedly. Then the sun poured forth again; Lucas stretched because he had to get going to the gym; but the kitchen did not look the same. Mr. Deerfelt opened his eyes wide, and slowly squirmed upright.

"'Who cares'?" Mr. Deerfelt asked. He lifted himself into a standing position. "'Who cares'?" he asked again, looming over the table. "This is who cares," he said, and he reared back his head and began to squeal in a loud and terrifying manner. He stood there and he squealed, and while he squealed he stomped the floor with his good foot, and he kept on stomping the floor and squealing until at last he stumbled, heaved into the refrigerator, came down on the table with both elbows, then fell back into his chair, panting awhile with his tiny crocus going up and down until his breathing returned to normal.

Caroline walked Lucas to the door in silence, and she walked him down the steps and stood with him in the yard. She saw the shining bicycle, and she felt the sunlight on her hair and on her shoulders, and she smelled the yellow forsythia in the slight spring breeze. Then she took Lucas' two good hands in hers, and gracefully, grievingly, she kissed each palm.

HOW BIRDS SLEEP

She had already come at him with a knife and fork, and he had already swatted her in the eye, and she had already ripped his best pastel portrait of her in half, and he had already held her down on the floor till they both cried. Now, at 2 A.M., there was nothing they could do but take a walk. They looked at each other with all of their love that had backfired, and they could not cry anymore, and they could not smile, either, and they got up from the floor and walked down the circular staircase to the sidewalk.

This all took place a long time ago. They lived in a dorm. Outside the dorm, life seemed to have deserted them. Only the night was there: white clouds streaming past the moon. Tiny cold birds filled the trees, silent, watchful, and everyone in the college was sleeping as Seamus and Maggie stood rooted, utterly paralyzed as to which way to walk.

"I'll kill myself."

"Don't keep telling me that, Maggie."

"You bastard."

"I'm not a bastard, Maggie."

Finally they turned to the left and began to walk in the middle of the road.

It must have rained earlier because Thayer Street had a black gloss with white streaks in it where light from the street lamps had pooled up. Dim light came also from the closed shop windows across the street, but on the other side were only darkened windows, separate student windows with sleeping lovers inside: people trying so hard to drum up attachments to other people that when it came time to detach, they found the other people were in their fingernails and their cuticles and even in the backs of their throats and the pits of their stomachs.

Seamus thought he was going to be sick again.

"Don't be sick again, Seamus. Oh, honey. Darling."

Seamus stopped walking and closed his eyes and seemed to be breathing with his scalp. He reached out and took hold of one of Maggie's belt loops for balance.

They resumed walking. Seamus tried not to look sideways at the legs of his girlfriend in their forest-green tights because he pitied them. He had loved them for three years and now for no reason he pitied them and did not want to see them anymore. For no reason except that it was over.

"Please talk to me," she said, her face steaming with hope. "I want a conversation. All you give me is remarks."

"All I have is remarks."

"But you have conversations with other people."

Seamus seemed to be breathing for two. He looked at

the face of his first love and wondered why his very core felt pinched by her radiance, why those same lovely blond looks that had beckoned to him so passionately for three years were now suffocating to him. Why for three years he had worshipped the icy vapor that seemed to twirl off her eyes, virgin-blue like the Popsicles she loved, until the vapor disappeared, the eyes became cactus-blue, flat and empty of mystery. It was impossible to defend himself when he was as lost for answers as she was. He wiped a spot of rain from his temple, summoning his energy.

"What would you like to do?" he asked. "Would you like a snack at the Ivy Room? Would you like a Popsicle? They've got real fruit Popsicles made of juice instead of water in the Ivy Room. Or an ice-cream sandwich? Are you hungry?"

"Is the Ivy Room open?"

"Oh," said Seamus, turning and looking with renewed disappointment at the blackened windows of the building that housed the Ivy Room. "The Ivy Room must have closed hours ago."

"See, you leave me with an empty feeling," Maggie said, picking at the heel of her shoe, which had come unglued hours before. "May I say this as a friend? Can we forget everything for a minute and will you just understand when I say—"

"What?"

Maggie waved her hands—never mind. Never mind. Never mind.

They turned left on George Street. They were so weary of battling each other all day and night that they walked up the middle of the road bumping into each other.

"Not so much an empty feeling," Maggie said at last, "as a feeling that everything was given to me and now everything has been ripped away. Like your pastels. All your artwork leaves the same feeling." Seamus was about to ask her why then for God's sake wouldn't she let him leave, but she waved her hands again. Never mind.

Earlier, in the bright daylight of noon, he had tried physically running from her. He had run across the Green and hid behind the statue of Marcus Aurelius. Then, after she had broken her heel finding him, he had tried running again and locking himself in his room, but she had sat in the public courtyard below and had called up to his window.

"Don't you know we love each other," she had called, "and that this break-up is wrong? And I don't care who hears. Breaking up is really wrong. I don't want to ask you anymore . . . but nights will be bad! I'm so scared, Seamus; I hate to say please, or to beg—but I think we are wonderful together. I love you very much and I don't ever want you to forget it, no matter what happens. I love you in my sleep! I love you more! I love you so much I could cry . . . with happiness!"

Then she had begun to weep about how birds sleep and Seamus had come down and opened the door for her—pitiful snot-faced child. That was not how she wanted to be remembered, was it? As an orphan, a war orphan or worse, a love orphan with no one to turn to, nobody to care for her, least of all herself? But she didn't care. She didn't care. She wanted Seamus to be so close that he didn't care, either.

Now, under the wet sycamore trees of George Street, Maggie said, "I'm so sleepy, Seamus, but I don't want to sleep. I don't want to be ignorant of what I feel. I'm going to do something bad, Seamus; I feel that I'm close to doing something awful to myself."

"Sweetheart, there's nothing I can do to stop you."

"What do you mean, you can't stop me? Don't you care?"

"I care."

"Then do something."

"Like what?"

Maggie turned on him again. *"Love me!"* she screamed—and tore at his ears, his hair, his cheeks, spitting and flailing like a madwoman. Seamus was stronger. He pinned her arms behind her and held her legs between his like a vise. "Ow," she whimpered—and, as he expected, tried to bash upward with her knee.

Suddenly she was down in a street puddle on both knees, clasping his thighs and burying her tears in his groin. "I'm sorry, I'm sorry, I'm sorry," she whispered reverently. "Oh, tell him not to go," she prayed, as though to an icon. "Tell him not to leave me. *You* don't want to leave me, do you?"

Seamus struggled to get her to stand.

"No, no, no," she whispered. Then shrieked: "What do you want to do with other girls? What is it you want to do?" And she postulated a number of desperate things that Seamus had never expected to hear from the mouth of his first love. Then she began to sob again, shaking and suffering, and Seamus had to stand there in the empty street for some time with two arms around his legs. They had the dripping sycamore trees to themselves, with the salty breeze blowing off the bay. They were all alone.

There were things, Seamus realized, *things in the world you should not do. Things you had to avoid doing. Take a duckling from its mother was one of the things you should avoid doing at all cost—for if you handled a duckling and then tried to give it back to its mother, the mother would peck it to death. I don't know why the mother would do that,* Seamus thought—*she just would. Or leave a pet rabbit outside in its cage so that a dog barked at it. If you let a caged rabbit get barked at, even if it was perfectly safe in its cage, it would begin to shake and shake and pretty soon it would drop over dead.*

Why is that?

I don't know.

Could you hold a butterfly by its wings? Seamus tried to remember. *No,* he decided, standing in the street with the salty breeze blowing off the bay—*that was another thing you had to beware of: The butterfly would thereafter lose its ability to fly.*

How many things were there to avoid doing in the world?

Hard to say. At least two hundred.

Give milk to a stray kitten?

Oh, yes.

Sleep with a virgin?

Oh, yes. That was one of the two hundred. You had to be extremely careful not to give milk to a stray kitten, or sleep with a virgin. You had to leave stray kittens and virgins alone to do whatever they had to do by themselves. You had to take no part. You had to be restrained—more restrained than you ever knew you had to be. When you were born, you never knew how restrained you had to be. When you were ten, you never knew it.

But if you did not know it by the time you were twenty, Seamus thought, *you'd be one of the lucky oafs who never knew.*

Seamus looked down at Maggie, with her head up in supplication, her eyes closed, her face dreamy with awe, her forest-green tights getting sopped in the puddle and one shoe broken at the heel.

"Tell me again how birds sleep?" he heard her ask.

Seamus helped her to stand. He put his arms around her and turned them both left onto Brown Street, where paper notices for roommates rustled damply from their thumbtacks on the tree trunks.

"Birds have tendons," Seamus began, "that run from their

feet right over their knees. When birds are tired, and they begin to slump, their knees bend and pull the tendons taut, making the claws in their feet clench. That's how birds can sleep standing up, clinging to branches and telephone wires without falling off."

They walked under glistening branches. Swollen beads of water dripped around them from on high like lazy bombs.

"You mean as the bird gets drowsier and heavier, its body works to fasten it on even better," Maggie said. "I love that idea."

Seamus was crying silently, but he didn't let her see.

"Is it my turn to tell *you* how birds sleep?" she asked him.

Seamus didn't say anything for a minute. Then he coughed to cover his tears.

"It's ingenious," Maggie said. "Birds have these tendons . . ."

How did they do it, again?

How they did it, see, was that Maggie would burst into tears while they were making love. A hundred times she would burst into tears of joy or yearning—deeply ancient sobs of trust as he continued to press upward—and afterward she would sigh and smile and ask him to tell her the story again. It was her favorite story to listen to and to tell back to him. Lying there with her tears drying on his shoulder, a hundred times she would listen to how the tendons would tighten with the birds' body weight, pulling the claws tighter. An ingenious idea. Therefore the deeper the birds slept, the tighter their claws would cling. A mythical idea. She would kiss him then, a hundred times. And then she would fall asleep, dreaming that she was a bird, slumping into him, holding him tighter as she slept.

Softly, after a few minutes in the darkness of Brown Street, Seamus loosened her grip on his arm.

19

And after another few minutes Maggie softly said, "Do you understand why I have to kill myself?"

"Tell me," Seamus said.

"Because I don't ever want to get over you. I don't ever want time to heal the wound."

"You know that's what would happen?"

"Indeed," Maggie said. "That's the scariest thing of all. It means I can't even trust myself to go on hurting . . ."

Maggie breathed evenly, in and out. "I'm very lucid right now. I know not everyone gets destroyed over something like this. They change. It's amazing how easily they change. They wait awhile and sooner or later they fall out of love and fall in love with someone else, and sleep with them, and forget all about how birds sleep."

"It's amazing how they heal," Seamus agreed.

"I have to kill myself to keep that from happening. I never want to be that fickle."

"Change isn't fickleness," Seamus said.

"Yes, it is," Maggie said calmly. "That's exactly what it is. And you're not such a bastard that you don't know it, too."

Seamus snapped off a piece of watery twig as they continued walking. He pressed it to his lips.

"I guess I'm willing to take my chances," he said.

"I guess you are," Maggie said. "What do you care, if one day your heart and soul stand for one thing, and the next day it's all backward, and your heart and soul stand for something else . . ."

"It's bad to fall out of love," Seamus admitted. "But it's not bad enough for me to kill myself."

"No one's asking you to kill yourself, Seamus."

"No?"

"I hope your next girlfriend dies," Maggie said then. "If that's what you want—to be free to see other girls, to marry someone else someday—go ahead, and I want her to die. And I hope your children die, too—in a tidal wave! I hope they die by drowning—like I am right now."

Suddenly she turned to him in a kind of rapture.

"Please let's just go and kill ourselves," she begged, pulling the skin around her eyes tight so the blue eyeballs bulged forth. "Please let's just go back to your room and wrap our legs around each other and not say another word and just do it. Don't leave me! Don't leave me! Or give me a baby so I can kill myself and be together with your baby inside me forever! Oh, Seamus, Seamus, am I desperate?" she wailed, from a faraway pulsating place. "Is this what it feels like to lose the whole world?"

Seamus stopped walking. They were on the street in front of Andrews House, the infirmary.

"Stay here," he told Maggie. "Or come inside, if you want. But I have to see a doctor."

He seemed to be having trouble breathing again.

"Are you all right?" Maggie asked.

"I need to talk to someone."

"Oh," she said, pausing. "Not me?"

"Not you."

"I adore you, Seamus."

"I know that, darling."

Radiant with despair, Maggie sat on a nearby stone bench and began to pick at her heel again.

Seamus climbed the two marble steps to the door and pressed the night bell beside the heavy iron-and-glass door. After a long moment the door was pulled open by a nurse wearing such white clothes Seamus had to squint. It felt like many hours or days since he had seen a human being so bright.

"Is there a doctor on call?" Seamus asked.

"Did you hurt your eyes?"

21

"Someone's going to kill herself. Is there a doctor on call?"

The nurse turned crisply and scrambled ahead, gesturing him to sit in the waiting room. Presently a tall man came in wearing a white flannel jacket, also so very bright and gentle he seemed to have just been awakened from a dream or emerged from a blizzard. Seamus thought he was in the presence of Eskimos or angels, so grateful was he for company. But he knew that all they were were other people. It seemed so long.

Wet, disheveled, Seamus sat there in the presence of this doctor, and he poured out to him what was going on: how he had once loved Maggie, how he was hurting her, how he had picked up a butterfly by its wings and taken a duckling from its mother and given milk to a stray kitten and now—worst of all the two hundred things—how he was not letting birds sleep, maybe never letting them sleep again . . . because he was a bastard.

"You're not a bastard," the doctor said.

"I don't love her anymore," Seamus explained.

"You're not a bastard."

"I'm forcing her to kill herself," he insisted.

"How do you know she'll kill herself?"

"I know."

The doctor looked away. When he looked back at Seamus, incredibly, his eyes were moist. With the gentlest voice ever, the doctor said the toughest words ever:

"How dare you?"

And he was right—Seamus ought never to have presumed such a thing about a person. For the next half hour Seamus thought hard about that, as he went back outside and collected Maggie and they finished their walk. The whole next day he thought hard about it, as he drove her the hundred miles to her home and dropped her off in her driveway and backed away from her small screaming figure and left. Four months later he thought hard about it, when Maggie married a boy she'd known in high school, the son of an auto-parts magnate; and four years later, when she had her first set of twin boys; and fourteen years later, when she ran successfully for assistant district attorney on the Republican ticket in a large city in upper New York State. *It's amazing—*

What is?

—how people don't die.

AVOIDING THE
SHOALS OF PASSION

The plan was this: After the graduation ceremonies, Beverly would take her parents back to her room for twenty last minutes of packing, Otis would take his parents on a brief tour of the MIT campus, then both families would meet at eleven-thirty in front of the nuclear engineering laboratory and walk together to the sit-down delicatessen for lunch. (The delicatessen idea had been Otis' one contribution to the plan, and Beverly had agreed at once; it would help make Otis' parents feel at home. Also it was inexpensive, for whichever set of parents insisted on picking up the tab.) Then after lunch, say twelve-fifteen, or as late as twelve-thirty if the dark delicatessen beer put Otis' father in one of his toast-making moods, they would carefully arrange the luggage in the two cars and take off for

Beverly's family homestead in Franklin, two hours north on 93. There the parents could spend a couple of country hours getting to know each other before Otis and his parents headed back to Jersey. It was an eminently sensible plan conceived by eminently sensible people. Otis the astrophysics major and Beverly the computer-math major had shaken hands on it the night before. Only as an afterthought had it occurred to them to pucker their lips and blinkingly kiss—which was fine. In their four years of undergraduate life they both had seen enough relationships founder on the bizarre and treacherous shoals of passion that it was fine to base theirs on friendship and good sense.

The wedding itself was going to be harder to plan, or at least they thought one part of it was going to be harder: the urban part, figuring out how much it meant to Mr. and Mrs. Spizer that their son be married back home among their thousand good neighbors in Newark. From what she could gather, Beverly sensed that it would mean a great deal indeed, and for their sake she was willing to do the block party, the dancing in the streets, whatever it was they did in Newark—but Otis was more concerned for *her* parents, who were quiet country people, white-picket-fence country. Thus it was planned, and thus the plan worked out, that after a delicatessen lunch of corned beef and tongue (but no beer—the liquor license had been revoked), Beverly rode out toward Franklin with Mr. and Mrs. Spizer in the meat-smelling seats of their beat-up silver Cadillac, Otis rode with Mr. and Mrs. O'Day in the straw-filled windiness of their shiny pickup truck, and on the way what needed feeling out was felt.

By the time both vehicles rolled into the smooth ruts of the O'Days' driveway a marvelous thing had been established: Beverly's parents and Otis' parents were all of one heart that the only important thing was for Beverly and

Otis to be happy together and that all the rest of it—the "baloney on a bun" Mr. Spizer irreverently called it (he owned two butcher shops)—would fall into place wherever in the world it wanted to fall. It was remarkable. Beverly and Otis squeezed hands and then—right there in public between the pair of hot clacking autos—hugged. The two sets of parents beamed shyly at them, then came together themselves for the kind of embrace given only between people who are happily related or are planning to be happily related, the fathers clapping each other's back, the mothers kissing each other's cheek, and at their feet the O'Day chickens pecking at the tires of the unfamiliar silver Cadillac. Then it was time to be shy once again, people pulling apart and falling into the roles of guest and host, when suddenly Mr. Spizer shouted, "And now do I get to see your horse?" And, turning to Beverly, he planted a fleshy kiss upon her mouth, making her cringe the tiniest bit. Everyone else thought that it was an exuberant but sweet thing for this tiny, dimpled man to do. Beverly decided to smile.

Turning on his heel, throwing his arms open wide at the cloudless sky, the barn buildings, the tractor in the distant sunlight under a trio of white butterflies, Mr. Spizer cried, "I love this backwoods setting!" He flipped a jumbo-sized handkerchief out of his breast pocket and dangled it over his head while he kicked the air a number of times in a fancy little dance step that made everyone laugh, including Beverly. Then, with no warning, he stopped in his tracks and used the handkerchief to blow his nose, making everyone look away. Beverly looked at Otis but he was taking his mother by the arm and in a second all of them were walking toward the farmhouse.

On the porch they ate cherry pie, homemade, of course, served on wooden plates with the thickest white napkins Beverly had ever seen her mother use. Mr. O'Day looked proud of the pie and the plates in his bashful, red-eared way. He was using the best manners Beverly had ever seen him use. Mr. Spizer preferred not to sit in the high-backed Shaker chairs occupied by everyone else, but rocked in the very old and fragile rocking chair in rhythm with his enthusiastic chewing. Four times Mr. Spizer told Mrs. O'Day how very delicious was her cherry pie, how much better than anything you could get in Newark, and then he grilled her as to what was in it, smiling and nodding very attentively as she listed her ingredients, though Beverly could tell he knew not a thing about baking. Finally, when Mrs. O'Day's cheeks were pink with the unaccustomed flattery, Beverly watched as Mr. Spizer turned his strange but rather charming curiosity onto the subject of the farm itself, in the form of quick, diverse questions to Mr. O'Day: How many acres did it have; was there a problem with insects; how could such a pretty little insect as a Japanese beetle cause the damage it did; was an acre bigger or smaller than an average city block, approximately? This last question was put to Mr. O'Day by Otis. Beverly was surprised.

They meant merely to pass through the bare, polished house on the way to the barnyard door, but the sixteen hanging photographs of Beverly as a child, before she had gotten spectacles, kept Otis and his father busy in the living room, their four brown shoes moving slowly side by side along the perimeter of the braided rug. "I didn't know she wore pigtails," Otis remarked at one point, and Mr. Spizer replied, "Oh, what a nice-looking girl she's always been." And then the shoes went sidling along some more while everyone else passed beyond to the kitchen and the door they wanted. "Coming, gentlemen?" called Mrs. Spizer from the yard—it was clear that she was the strict one in the family—but it was nearly ninety seconds in the dusty sunlight before the group was once again complete.

Joining them with his jovial energy in this field that was called a backyard, Mr. Spizer clapped and rubbed his hands together as if a long-delayed treat was finally coming due. "Now to see the horse!" he said. "Yes?"

"Well, Beverly's mare can be jittery with newcomers," Mrs. O'Day said. "There are goats to see, or cows—"

There was a pause of black depression.

"We can see her if you'd like," Mrs. O'Day said.

Joy! Commotion!

"Is she truly dangerous?" Mr. Spizer asked Beverly as he danced along to the horse barn under the tidy blue sky. "How long have you had her?" Otis came up along Beverly's other side and looked at her with a similar eagerness. "Can you believe we've graduated today?" he said. "What did you do with your cap and gown?"

"I packed them in my book bag," Beverly told Otis. "Yes," she told Mr. Spizer, "she can be dangerous, if you don't handle her right." Beverly watched the way Mr. Spizer was lifting his brown shoes high out of the grass with each step, as if he didn't want to trample on any of the multitudinous wildlife that might live therein.

"Our whole lives ahead of us!" Otis suddenly shouted.

They were at the horse barn. It was a square building set under a large locust tree that filtered the light down through the leaves in a soft way. Beverly noticed that Mr. Spizer ducked under the leaves as if they were part of a plastic awning, something to keep the rain off one's head. When they got inside she kept an eye on Mr. Spizer because he seemed to be having trouble adjusting to the darkness. Beverly's mother cautioned Mr. Spizer to stay on the mare's left side, always on the left. The mare was fidgety with everyone crowded into the stall. Beverly went around front and kissed her nose hello, kissed her big humorless eyelids. Mr. Spizer asked Mrs. O'Day if he could touch, and when he got the go-ahead he placed his fingertips on her neck with great respect, as if it constituted an especially sharp-bladed cleaver. "Ah," he said, "so smooth," and he smiled, and everyone smiled. He wanted to touch the tail, and Mrs. O'Day let him do that, too. Mrs. O'Day showed him the hair in swirls on the torso, and the knobs on the knees, and the pressure points on the ankles. She went on to explain about the care and upkeep of the hooves, lifting one of the hooves and demonstrating, with two fingers, how the mealy underside should be ground out daily to prevent rot. Mr. Spizer giggled slightly with surprise to find a horse and a hoof and a hand so suddenly nearby him in the heat of the countryside. "What must it all smell like?" he asked, and without waiting for a reply he grabbed Mrs. O'Day's fingers and put them to his nostrils.

"Oh, like after you cut your toenails," he said.

Such an innocent thing to say! Yet Beverly's mother looked at Beverly's father, both looked at Otis' mother, who looked at Otis, who looked, with a sheepish smile, at Beverly, and it was at this moment that Beverly understood she would never marry Otis.

THE GOOD-BYE PRESENT

1. How did Roy's wife react when Roy said, "This? This here's an elk tree," and slapped the bark authoritatively?

Roy's wife did not say a word or change her expression. But she felt victorious. Rita invariably felt victorious when her husband faltered, or made a mistake, or made a fool of himself. She was always prepared for victory of this type, and so she wore an expression of patient, queenly sufferance whenever she listened to him. Behind this frozen expression she waited passionately for her husband to stumble. Even if he were telling a funny story which happened to amuse her, Rita would project the pleasant, bored air of having endured the story a hundred times before. It was as if she were saying to everyone else, "You think he's charming, but put up with it as long as I have. . . ." And then when he made a mistake she'd be proved right—all she had to do was hold the expression, it was proof.

2. *Surely this was not a funny story he was telling?*

Correct. He was answering a question about a tree's identity.

3. *In what way was his answer a mistake?*

There is no such thing as an elk tree. There are elms and there are oaks.

4. *Did Rita always feel better after this sort of victory?*

Always. Rita was not a ham like her husband, so this was how she competed: counting minutes before he stumbled, waiting, waiting; and gloating sweetly once he did. Hearing him say "elk tree" was particularly gratifying. Silently, and without batting an eyelash, she cherished the moment he said it, and wished deeply that the moment would freeze, that everyone could stay as they were for eternity; she would love them all then, even Roy. Please freeze!

5. *Did God answer her prayer?*

There is no God. Rita was just a bad winner.

6. *Was she born that way?*

She was not born that way. She was not even married that way. Rita began to exult in each of her husband's mistakes, and secretly to rejoice every time something unfortunate happened to them as a couple, only when it became evident they were getting more than their share of bad luck. Her early hysterectomy. Adopted son turning out poorly. Roy's career as a songwriter washed up prematurely. All this would have been spooky had Rita allowed herself to be surprised each time. Instead she grew to accept misfortune, to anticipate and to welcome it.

7. *She was bitter?*

Not in the ordinary sense. She specialized in misfortune and derived satisfaction from it. There is a popular expression for this strategy.

8. *If you can't lick 'em, join 'em?*

Precisely. She joined 'em with glee. It was almost a game, it became her way of winning. It was like those card games where certain cards were bad, they counted against you . . . unless you got all of them. Then they were very valuable.

9. *Then Rita was ugly as a witch?*

On the contrary. She was bewitchingly beautiful. The more bad things she collected—husband mistakes, family tragedies, and so on—the more beautiful she became. On the day in question she wore a yellow ribbon in her black hair. She glowed with a negative electricity.

10. *What kind of day was it?*

The second day of the hottest weekend in years. The day before, Saturday, had been so bad that factories and offices up and down the Eastern seaboard were forced to close, suburban families to spend the weekend sitting in glacial shopping malls. Saturday night was even worse because of a blackout in New York City. All night thousands of half-delirious New Yorkers flocked to the Staten Island ferry for a ride through moving air, and by dawn Sunday mad schemes of escape had been concocted. One young couple on Manhattan's Riverside Drive awoke so faint that they hastily made arrangements to show up at Roy's place in Westhampton. As well as to catch an ocean breeze, they came to say good-bye.

11. How did Roy like that?

Roy loved his niece Henrietta; he could do without Henry. He did not like that they were moving the next day to Cambridge, England. He did not like that they were to pursue their doctorates. He thought they were overschooled already. They were. But their appearance in Westhampton was convenient because Roy had a good-bye present for Henrietta.

12. How did they react to Roy's identification of the elk tree?

They were sticky with embarrassment. However, they were often and easily embarrassed these days. Partly it was because Henrietta had recently learned that she was carrying their first child; they felt particularly impressionable, as if outside events could not only have an unnatural effect on themselves but could jinx the embryo, as well. Consequently they were often and easily bullied. Just the evening before, for instance, they had been bullied by a (hot and harried) barmaid on Bleeker Street. "Don't you have any food?" asked Henry when no menu had arrived with their second drinks. "How was I supposed to know you wanted to eat?" parried the barmaid effectively, giving them an order form to fill out. "Two spring chickens," Henrietta wrote. They laughed and blushed at the meaning.

"Three spring chickens" would have summed it up, for there was no doubt the progeny of such a gentle couple would be of the same cast: plump, pale, scholastic.

13. How do you know? There's no God . . .

I'm playing, playing. The progeny tried to kill himself over his first girlfriend nineteen years later. He tried to kill himself over his divorce thirty years later. He let a tour bus strike his wife dead in Piccadilly Circus fifty years later. He was brought up British.

34

14. Is it fun playing?

Eh.

15. Why didn't Henrietta correct her uncle about the elk tree?

She had no right to contradict him. She lost that right when she allowed him to love a heightened image of herself, a Henrietta far more merry, adorable, witty and surprising than the one she happened to be. She couldn't help it. Roy made her feel phony when she was most her true self. "I didn't mean it as a pun," she'd protest halfheartedly after he'd misconstrue one of her sentences; Roy would look at her sideways, see no livelier way the sentence could have been intended, think her all the more clever for protesting, and laugh with renewed appreciation. She would acquiesce, but it cost her her rights. If she couldn't stick up for her true self, she had no right to stick up for the rest of reality, including trees. An elk tree was just as real as the Henrietta she allowed to exist.

Henrietta guessed that Roy had heightened images, queenly but disturbed images, of all his women friends. It was his way of flirting with women and ultimately of ruling them. Henrietta always ended up feeling haggard and dull in the shadow of what he supposed her to be.

16. Why didn't Henry correct Roy?

Physical cowardice.

Roy ruled men by sheer might, and it was apparent that he would relish an excuse to make mincemeat of Henry. He was always wanting to lock horns with Henry. He would interrupt the younger man, closing in with his colossal chest and saying, "Aha! You mean . . ." and twisting what Henry had said. Then he'd ruffle Henry's hair or playfully take a swing at him and the argument would be over. And soon the next argument would begin. Henry sensed that Roy did not keep male friendships very long, that sooner or later he would have to prove himself mightiest, that he'd have to start pushing. He wouldn't be able to stop until he made his friend feel like a fairy.

17. *Was Henry losing his hair?*

And how. It wasn't to be ruffled.

So if Roy wanted to think there was such a thing as an elk tree, that was all right by Henry.

18. *To sum up, Roy's identification of the elm or oak as an elk tree was received in silence?*

Wrong! But to see where you made your mistake, it may be useful to rewind our tale to the wee hours of the morning.

Roy awoke with a familiar but ghastly pain in his chest. Carefully he took himself out of the bedroom, out of the house, and across the dark yard. He slumped in the middle seat of the family station wagon and groaned in privacy for an hour until the sun came up and the pain subsided. Thereupon he walked into the house and put on the kitchen radio softly. When Rita came downstairs he was fixing an omelet with chopped ham, green peas and red pepper. Rita activated the oven fan and removed herself to the living room, where twelve pillows were lying in wait for their Sunday fluffing. She went around the room giving each pillow four wallops, little by little loosening her yellow blouse from her black short-shorts. By her fourth pillow she had worked up a sweat above her lip, and by her sixth pillow she had worked up a rage. Physical activity first thing in the morning, when what she really wanted to do was lounge in bed, could always be counted upon to rouse some rage. She did it to herself deliberately, as if she were two people, one a sleepy-headed camper and the other a bugle-mouthed counselor on a campaign to make life miserable for all spoiled slugabeds. Rise and shine, you pampered bitch! Eight, nine, ten—each pillow was socked harder than the last—and the twelfth was carried furiously into the kitchen. "Will you please wake our darling young son!" she demanded over the racket of the fan.

Roy took the skillet with its bubbling omelet up to Ricky's room. "Oh, Ricky boy . . ." he sang to the tune of "Danny Boy," waving the dish, filling the dark, draped bedroom with an adventurous odor, ". . . your parents want you dow-hown stairs." "Ugh," said Ricky. "Oh yes, they do . . ." began the father again, ". . . or they will fry your fa-an-ny," humorously touching the skillet to the appointed mound in the blankets. "Leave me alone!" snarled the boy, turning his head to the wall, "I'll be down in a minute." Roy started to leave as there came, from under the pillow, an exclamation like a defiant "Good night!"— but lewd.

His chest seized up and Roy hurried out of the room.

The morning heated; telephone arrangements were made to receive refugees from Riverside Drive; at around eleven the not-quite-sporty Datsun crunched up the driveway with Henrietta at the wheel and Henry looking nervous; Bloody Marys and sardine finger-sandwiches were served under the leaves on the patio. "You're turning into a regular boozer," Roy told Henry sarcastically at eleven-thirty. "It's quite spicy," gasped Henry. At eleven forty-five Henrietta commented favorably on the patio's absence of mosquitoes. "That may be true," answered Rita, smacking her fingertips, "but there are enough spiders to make up for them." At noon Roy stood up. "Give your baby a good first name," he told his guests sonorously, "and then give it a better middle one." (The statement was not supposed to mean anything, necessarily, it was just supposed to sound sonorous.) Roy and Henrietta left the shade to play horseshoes. The percussive sounds from the sunny, close-cropped lawn continued for half an hour while Rita and Henry made political chitchat marked by a near-perfect shortage of facts and mutually agreeable conclusions. By twelve-thirty their conversation had turned personal. Rita asked him—clang! a howl and a squeal told her a rematch was to begin—how his doctoral program was set up, if he looked forward to the baby, did he feel sad about leaving the States, why he kept his shirt on in such weather. In reply to the last, Henry lowered his shirt and showed her the painful heat blisters on his shoulders; Rita shuddered, gaped, dared to touch . . . finally her breath trembled so strangely at the sight of the injury that she went inside to make another batch of Bloodys. A leaf floated down onto Henry's head. Rita returned with nail polish on the tray and began to apply it to one hand, then the other. "Roy always lets me win," wailed Henrietta from the horseshoe pit. "Nonsense!" bellowed Roy, reaching the patio suddenly and dropping himself onto his stool, "I let no one win! Ever!" They nibbled and drank. They perspired, all four: Roy steamed, shaking his massive head and sprinkling everyone; Rita seemed cool but, oppressed by her husband's reappearance, occasionally sighed at an oversized drop of sweat that tumbled down from the yellow ribbon at her hairline; Henrietta took Henry's soggy hand in her soggy hand. Peace and balance reigned for a quarter hour until, toward one o'clock, a second leaf landed on Henry's head. Looking up, Henry managed to spill the leaf and to study the branch whence it came. "Is this a hickory?" he mused. "This?" said Roy, slapping the bark authoritatively, "this here's an elk tree."

There was no "silence."

Ricky boy had arisen.

Question carefully.

19. What was Ricky wearing?

A purple bathrobe and purple slippers. Black-frame glasses over his orange bangs. A scowl. In his position on the upstairs deck he looked like a figurehead on the prow of a haunted ship.

20. Ricky slept until one?

Even at one he was not happy about rising. Experts say this is rare for twelve-year-old boys, but it was typical of Ricky, who suffered nightmares in the dark and frequently could not get to sleep until two, three, even four A.M. The night before he had stayed up extra late, pacing, reading, and finally passing off at about the time Roy was getting up.

21. Reading?

Monster paperbacks. And drawing monster pictures, gluing monster models, chewing monster bubble gum. It was Ricky's way of working out his nightmares. During the day he didn't have to be so quiet and was able to create imaginative monster sounds on his father's quadriphonic tape recorder. Remember that Roy was a songwriter and you will see what a distortion, what an affront Roy considered this last practice to be.

22. Sounds like little Ricky needed help, yes?

But where was he to get it? He was pretty certain his parents were monsters, and he was convinced, after one session, that the school psychologist was one of them too— else how could the guy know so much about them? Ricky protected his secrets from these dissemblers. If they asked about his preoccupation, he'd explain that he loved monsters, that monsters were his friends—a sensible lie, one curries favor where one can. If they asked him to name his favorite color, he'd say lime green, his least favorite. If

39

they asked him to make his bed, he'd tuck the quilt in crossways. Ricky was safer when he kept others off balance in these ways, but he blanched if they managed to throw him off balance. His world was perilous enough without people playing games, tampering with words, merging concepts, and saying things like "elk tree." Thus his scowling appearance on the upstairs deck, thus his pronouncement that his father was an "old drunk."

23. *That's what happened?*
Excuse me?

24. *That's what happened when Roy identified the tree?*
Yes.
"You old drunk!" said Ricky.
Rita looked up from her nail polish and turned to the two guests to reveal her wondrously mild expression. "Isn't this pleasant," it seemed to say, "wouldn't it be excellent to hear this day in and day out, as I do?"
Henrietta squeezed Henry's hand.
Roy said: "What. Did. You. Say?"
"You heard me," said Ricky, tittering a bit with excitement.
"WHAT?"
"An elk tree," said Ricky derisively, trying to expand the dialogue.
"Did you call me what I think you did?" asked Roy.
Ricky got the upper hand. "Probably," he said. "Hi, Cousin Henrietta, hi, Cousin Henry."
The cousins looked to Rita for directions on how to reply. Her face was wondrously mild and blank. "G'morning," they said.
"It's not morning," thundered Roy, "it's one o'clock in the afternoon. That's what time this big man gets up to take his breakfast!"

"Did you have a nice ride out here, Cousin Henry?" asked Ricky.

"Leave them out of it!"

Ricky's expression slowly changed from one of concern to one of grief. "I'm just trying to talk to my 'relatives,'" he told his father mournfully. "Good-bye, Henry and Henrietta," he said, turning to shuffle into the house.

"Ricky!" said Roy. "I would like an apology this minute."

"Don't you even want me to get dressed?" cried Ricky, vexed at every turn.

"I'm only going to say it two more times," warned Roy quietly.

"All right, I'm going," Ricky sighed.

"Apologize."

Ricky opened the door to the house.

"Apologize!" Roy burst to his feet.

Ricky let go of the door and watched it pump shut. With his head down and his hands in the pockets of his bathrobe, he shuffled back to his podium. "I'm sorry I told everyone that you were an old drunk, Daddy," he sniffed.

But that's what his daddy was turning into.

25. Roy was turning into an old drunk?

So I have said.

With all due respect, I must warn you not to waste questions.

26. Don't I get as many questions as I like?

This may come as a surprise. You get fifty questions altogether. Theoretically, we could go on and on, but fifty should give you an ample chance to get the complete story provided you don't waste any more of them.

27. How did I know to ask the first question about something called an elk tree and someone named Roy?

That question was given to you free, compliments of the house. Since then you've been on your own—and done magnificently.

28. *Was the way in which Roy and Rita met prophetic?*

The way every husband and wife meet is prophetic.

Roy and Rita met through a fun-loving, warm-hearted anatomy professor named Professor Abel. Roy took Professor Abel's introductory course as a requirement for freshmen. It met at eight A.M. One day Roy came to class with a hangover. Professor Abel asked Roy to stand and to recite all the bones in a human being's lower body. Roy included the penis. The professor thought this was hilarious and he went out of his way to befriend Roy. Six years later Rita, a coed without a hangover, made the same error. The professor couldn't get over it. He traced Roy through the alumni office and urged his two pupils to meet. Being young, they were good sports about it. They met, they laughed at how outlandish it was, they laughed some more, they romanced, they eloped and moved to Hollywood, where Roy was beginning a decade of prominence in the music field.

29. *Did this beginning portend of things happy or sad?*

Sad. The fact that the penis is boneless was crucial to the decay of their relationship.

30. *Are you saying Roy became impotent?*

Let's say he did not feel good about himself once his songs began to dry up. Rita became more beautiful every year, like a flame that blazes most brightly on its last bit of fuel, if you will.

31. *Whom did longtime friends consider to be at fault in the marriage, Roy or Rita?*

Nearly everyone believed that Rita was emerging as the

good soul in the marriage, that Roy—with his drinking, his bad-natured outbursts, his overly large mannerisms— was showing his true colors. Even people who liked Roy best were surprising themselves by coming to this con- clusion.

One of the only persons to know better was the anat- omy professor. He was no longer a "friend" because Roy had taken offense at something or other long ago, but from what reports he could get, the good professor sur- mised that Rita was the villain. In his view Rita took Roy's penis-bone, she took his backbone, she took his ribs—she filleted him. And all because life wasn't working out per- fectly, beginning with the hysterectomy and then the other setbacks, and she had to make bad worse. She wanted a clean sweep of badness. The professor thought Rita to be a powerful and dangerous woman. He was cor- rect. The wondrous mildness she displayed in times of stress, the inner calm, the patience, was not that of some- one who was bearing up under terrible odds, but of a sated despoiler. She had collected nearly all the bad cards and now she could afford to relax.

32. *What did Roy do after Ricky apologized?*

He muttered "Ricky, Ricky, Ricky," and then he ad- dressed his pregnant niece and said, "It's still worth it— with all the heartache, and with all the . . . crap! . . . it's still worth it," and then to Henry: "You remember that." And then looking up at the tree, he hummed the melody to "Try to Remember," and then he faced Rita with new energy and sang, "Try to remember that this, is an elk tree, it is, just that, because, I—say—so," and then he switched to bourbon. This entailed his walking into the house.

33. *Did anything transpire in his absence?*

You bet. While Roy was getting the bourbon, Rita quietly told the two youngsters that Roy had lung cancer.

They said, "What!" And Henrietta added, "Can anything be done?"

"Since he found out about it he refuses to see any doctors," Rita said, screwing closed the skyscraper cap of the nail polish with fingers that needed to dry. She was plainly wearied of the way Roy handled real-life situations. "Your uncle thinks that would be giving in to it, you see."

The door opened and Ricky, who knew nothing of this matter, approached with the bourbon tray. He still wore his bathrobe and slippers. Rita said, "Oh, I thought you were your father."

"No," said Ricky, "my father's on the potty." As he leaned to set down the tray he grunted emphatically, by way of rounding out the picture.

"So that's the latest," Rita concluded, taking a sip from Roy's glass.

"I can't believe it," said Henrietta.

"Neither can I," said Henry.

"Why not?" interrupted Ricky. "Everybody's got to go sometime. Sometimes when he has to go number one, he does it right out here."

Rita sputtered into her husband's drink, a short laugh. "That's disgusting," she said lightly, wiping the side of the glass and relegating it to the arm of Roy's chair.

"I just think it's horrible," reaffirmed Henrietta.

"Same here," said Henry. "Cut it out," he told Ricky, who had taken a seat at his feet and was harmlessly tossing patio pebbles up onto his lap.

"No, but this is really, really horrible," said Henrietta. "Do you think," she asked Rita, "I could be of any help if I talked to him?"

"He'll most likely tell you it's nothing, a virus," she answered. "An elk virus."

"I know what you mean," interrupted Ricky. They turned to him with alarm. "He's crazy. He really thinks this is an elk tree, just because he wants it to be. Somebody," he said, tossing up three larger pebbles, "should really call his bluff sometime."

The grown-ups thought about that for a couple of minutes. Finally Rita said, "Oh, go away, Ricky."

34. *What was taking Roy so long?*

Sad to report, Roy was feeling sorry for himself on the john. It began when he noticed the guest towels beside him, lovely towels with blue and brown Peruvian designs. He recalled that he had bought them for Rita long ago in Hollywood. In the store the towels had been stiff and coarse, but Roy figured they would soften with a few washings. It had seemed to him that the towels were too expensive to remain stiff and impractical. Young, newly rich, in love, the songwriter believed money was like that: It would automatically buy you things that were both lovely to look at and practical, too. But the towels never softened. They remained completely useless, scratchy. Roy's life seemed to him a folly.

Roy drew three sheets of toilet paper from the spool. He held the first one, the farthest one, in his hand.

"Damn it already, Ricky!" he heard. It was Henry yelling. Henry had jumped up and brushed the pebbles from his lap onto Ricky's face. "Enough already!"

Roy pulled on the farthest sheet. It ripped inadequately. Instead of getting all three sheets, he only got part of one. A sob of outrage, at things both great and small, came out of Roy. Immediately he snapped back, he regained control—but this was a very frustrated man.

35. *Isn't it unusual for a successful man to act like that?*

I'm afraid not very. You should have seen him earlier in the middle seat of the station wagon.

36. *Was Roy now a better gift-buyer than he had been in Hollywood?*

Not in Henrietta's view. All the gifts she had ever received from Roy, from the shocking Arabic perfume he gave her in first grade, to the Danish hand mirror of last Christmas, were inappropriate; they managed to make Henrietta feel insufficient. The hand mirror was royal, but Henrietta was not; it was a fantasy she could not live up to. The sight of her chubby, unproud face reflected in the Danish oval, framed by silver swan figurines, revolted Henrietta; it made her feel homely by contrast, a fat duck. She felt odd when she used it, as if she were part of a frightening fairy tale—worshiped by a blind suitor or captured by a two-hundred-year-old prince.

Actually it was Roy who had captured her. He had forced the gift upon her, as he forced all his gifts, and she hadn't had the nerve to reject it. She couldn't bring herself to say, "Here, take it back. You've got me all wrong. I don't like seeing myself this way." Dutifully she took the mirror and dutifully she kept it on her dresser. And every time she looked in it she was his prisoner, she was his princess, as surely as if he had molded a silver crown around her head.

37. *Did Roy ever buy things for himself?*

From time to time. He didn't scrimp on himself except when important matters were at stake, such as his health.

38. *Why wouldn't Roy see a doctor for his cancer?*

A. He preferred to think of it not as cancer but as a cigarette pain. He had quit smoking already; what more could a doctor prescribe?

B. He had a superstition that he'd be a goner if he underwent an operation. He knew it was irrational but he feared that the open air would "stimulate" the cancer.

39. *Two excuses?*

But of course. Every bad move Roy made was supported by at least two excuses, so that if something should happen to one, he would be held steady to his error by the other. He refrained from locking the bathroom door, for instance, on the grounds that (*a*) he might find himself lacking some item and have to call out for it, and (*b*—in which he was very much a child of his time) he considered locking the bathroom door a sign of paranoia.

40. *In what way was this a bad move?*

People generally do not like their niece's husbands to surprise them in the bathroom.

41. *Was Henry embarrassed about barging in?*

"Oops, sorry!" he exclaimed. "I just came in to wash my face! It's so humid! Boy! I'll let you finish!"

"That would be grand of you, Henry," said Roy.

Naturally he was embarrassed, but worse was to come a minute later when Roy passed him in the kitchen. "Sorry about that," he said, rinsing his face with a moist paper napkin.

"About what?" said Roy. "I've already forgotten it." He began to pour himself a Scotch.

"Oh, I think," ventured Henry, dabbing around his neck, "I think your bourbon is waiting for you on the patio."

"Lucky me," said Roy. "Well, I guess I can handle the both of them."

"'Lucky Me,'" repeated eager, wire-brained Henry. "Wasn't that the name of your first hit song?"

Roy was well pleased. But he looked as if he were going to hit Henry.

"You big boozer," he said threateningly, putting down the drink. "You little rummy. Since when do you know about my past, you lush? Think you caught me being sentimental, making private jokes?" He came toward Henry with the wide, circling arms of a performing wrestler. "You have not lived until you have been in one of my famous four-hour headlocks."

"Wait, wait," gabbled Henry, uttering a laugh. "Ow, ow," he yelped just before Roy grabbed him by the neck and the waist and bent him like a fluffy pipe cleaner. "My blisters!"

Gently, manfully, Roy turned his advantage into a paternal hug. With one hand he buried Henry's head in his big shoulder, patting and rubbing. "I'd never hurt you," he told Henry in a voice thick with emotion, "you know I'd never hurt you. Henry," he said, rocking them both, "you're a good man, Henry. You're going to be a good father. And Henrietta"—he inhaled sharply—"she's going to be a wonderful mother . . . loving and kind and . . . beautiful as a queen. I want you to believe that. You believe that, don't you, Henry?"

"Sure," came the muffled, mortified voice of Henry, who was quickly formulating a cancer superstition of his own, namely, that cancer might be contagious at certain proximities.

Embarrassed? Yes, but Henry was used to that; far worse was feeling infected.

42. How did Henry deal with this new feeling?

By proceeding, directly upon his return to the patio, to get smashed.

43. Did this help?

It might have helped had Henry chosen an appropriate chair from which to do it, but he mistakenly chose a low-slung canvas chair situated below the level of the table. Henry was too inexperienced a drinker to know the connection between posture and mood, so he sprawled, he stewed, he half-snoozed as the heat collected, as the chatter peaked and peaked again, as Ricky chewed monster bubble gum at his ear. Cheese muffins were passed down to him. Brown apple slices were passed down to him. Conversation strayed into his space and was trapped. Henrietta offered to spray his feet with a hose; Henry waved off the treat; she sprayed elsewhere. Ricky created a ghoulishly green bubble nearby. Suddenly Henry took one drop past his limit. The stupor clutched him before he'd even had time to set his glass back down on the pebbles. The bubble grew closer, paler, larger; it filled his vision. Rita was enveloped; the elk tree squeezed in; Roy entered laughing, telling a serious Henrietta, "Not to worry about me, not to worry." Henry saw with dismay that the not-quite-sporty Datsun parked beyond the patio had also been swallowed up; it looked not-quite-capable of driving him out and away. For one long second Henry believed he was sitting in a cold tub, at his home on Riverside Drive . . . Sweating, he came to and pinpointed the handkerchief in his breast pocket.

"Are you all right?" asked the black-and-yellow lady.

"He looks unsocial," advised the purple boy.

"Henry," panted the wife.

Roy had an idea. "All right, everyone give him room," he instructed. "Henry, just relax and breathe normally. Ricky," he said evenly, "get that out of his face."

"It's just a bubble," explained Ricky. Nevertheless, it withdrew.

"Is he going to be all right?" Henrietta asked.

Roy chuckled. There was a wet, echoing chuckle from Henry.

The relief was too fast for Rita. She stared out to the horseshoe pit, then blinked back to her fingernails. "I must be quite a hostess," she sighed.

There was the sound of an airplane, invisible.

Roy stood Henry on his feet and proceeded to walk him around the premises. They stopped briefly at the bird bath, where Henry consented to douse his head, they spent a few minutes at the tomato patch, and then continued through the back door of the house.

44. Were they going anyplace in particular?

Roy led Henry to his music den. It looked like the fix-it area of a rich man's radio shop. The thick white broadloom was strewn with tape reels, breakable television components; the shelves were loaded with electronic machinery, tiny screwdrivers . . . and a small cardboard box that Roy took down. It was sealed with masking tape.

45. The good-bye present!

"This here is for Henrietta," he said. "Think you're steady enough to carry it?"

"In a minute," said Henry, lowering himself to the piano bench.

"I was going to scrub it with ammonia, but I decided that was the husband's job," Roy said. "It'll be priceless when you get the crime out."

"The what?"

"The cobwebs and grime," said Roy. "Whatever."

Henry struck middle C on the keyboard. "I feel somewhat better," he said.

Roy supported Henry by the elbow back to the patio. As they approached he whispered, "It's from one of Westhampton's great big mansions. I picked it up at a garage sale. Give it to her with a little buildup, you know?"

Obligingly, Henry placed the box on the table before

his wife. "This is from Roy," he said. "It may be a little dirty but it's supposed to be quite valuable."

"Oh, Roy," said Henrietta, delicately unpeeling the masking tape. "An antique?"

"Well, kind of," said Roy happily.

"That means junk," warned Ricky.

Before anyone could respond, Henrietta pulled out a tall crystal baby bottle. Her heart skidded. She could find nothing to say. One side of the interior was caked with fruity white cocoons. The nipple was cracked and moldy.

"I was just telling Henry that a little ammonia will clean it right up," chirped Roy. "Of course, you might want to replace the nipple. That's easy enough."

"Yes," said Henrietta slowly, "yes."

"You're unfocusing again," Roy told Henry.

There was a sweaty silence . . .

. . . But Rita, for once, was not inclined to cherish it. "Maybe Henrietta wanted to breast-feed, Roy."

Roy didn't like that. "I don't give a damn what she wants to do," he shouted. "She can use it for a juice bottle. Or what if the baby is a biter?" He was angry at his wife. "You've got to have a little imagination, damn it all!"

Henrietta had lost her color. She looked up at Roy.

"That's real crystal," he pointed out. "You'll have to be careful if you want to boil it. Now I know a lot of women like to have all new things for their first baby, and that's fine: I don't mind if you go out and get a hundred new bottles. I just thought it was important for you to have this, too."

"It's from an ancient kingdom," Henrietta breathed.

"There, you see!" crowed Roy. "Someone here's got a head on her shoulders."

Henrietta looked pleadingly at Rita. "But it's horrible!"

she said. "It's for a queen that's dead and buried! Can't you tell him that?"

"What in the hell is going on here?" said Roy. "Everybody's jinxed on account of a few little spiders have gotten in. Give it back if you don't like it. I'll trade it for a couple of art books or something. Jesus Christ, I'm telling you." He looked around for someone to tell.

"Why did you make me carry it out?" stammered Henry.

"Oh, shit," said Roy.

"Can I see it?" asked Ricky. Henrietta handed him the bottle.

"Dead, my foot," said Roy. "Who's got a cigarette?"

Ricky put the bottle to the light and studied it with detachment. "Daddy," he said reasonably, "it's secondhand."

"Well, so are you, buddy!"

Ricky continued studying the bottle.

"Forget that," said Roy very quietly. "It didn't mean anything. Please stop," he said. "Everyone stop thinking."

"It was a mistake," said Rita. "It didn't mean anything."

"That's right," Roy said. "People say things that are stupid and cruel and meaningless sometimes. And I'm no exception."

"It's all right," said Henrietta. "Sometimes things pop out of my mouth that don't mean anything. It happens to everybody."

"Silly, dumb things," said Roy. "The trouble is that people don't think before they speak."

"It's nothing to remember," said Henry. "It's easily forgotten."

"I think so, too," said Roy. "We'll forget it here and now. No need to spoil the afternoon. Whom can I help with another drink? Rita, some bourbon? Ricky," he said, turning to his son for the first time, "can I get you a glass of something?"

Thoughtfully Rick smashed the bottle down so that the crystal shards flew up and about like a shower of ice in the sunlight, turning red and blue and green. No one moved. No one spoke. The end.

46. *The end?*
The end.

47. *They just sat there, frozen?*
Frozen. Some more than others.

48. *Did time stand still?*
Yes. No. It seemed to, but slowly, gracefully, it reasserted itself. The afternoon had nearly passed.

49. *And Henry and Henrietta?*
After a while they began to talk about going. The heat was breaking up. The sun was going down. Still they sat amid the bits of broken crystal. The sunset was seen through the leaves of the elk tree. You might think the sunset after that infernal weekend was ghoulish, green, like a monster bubble. But it was radiant, pink . . .

It was their last sunset in the States. Next day they would leave for England forever.

50. *The sky radiant, ablaze with death, with new life, a hex broken, a baby on its way, arrival and departure! Isn't the world rich?*
The farewells took place in semidarkness. Rick did not trouble to come out of his father's den where he was engrossed in watching baseball on his father's large, and rather loud, television. Rita and Roy quietly walked their guests to the car. There was much solemn hugging, kissing and waving. A mile down the road Henrietta discovered she had left her purse behind. They drove back to the house and Henrietta walked inside. No one was around.

She located her purse. She stood around a moment and then called: "Good-bye again!" Roy came out of the den with a drink in his hand and a finger to his lips. "Shh," he said, "Rita's taking a rest." Then he hugged Henrietta once more, saying, "It'll be good. Don't worry. Even after everything . . ." Quietly he walked her to the front door and pressed their foreheads together under the lamplight. His eyes welled up. "I wish the world were dead," he told her.

KATEY FOSTER'S
TWO BOYS

"Would you like some of my roast beef?" Ellen asked.

"Thanks, no."

"It's really not too bad," Ellen said.

"No thanks, really."

"Don't you feel you deserve it? After fathering a second son?"

Toby yawned.

"I don't know *why* I'm so famished," Ellen said, sitting up in the bent white bed amid the profusion of flowers, and using so much energy to cut through the yellowish asparagus on her plate with her plastic fork that she actually scrunched up one side of her triumphant tired face.

About the flowers: The four dozen roses that Toby had insanely rushed out and bought, so that they would be in his wife's room by the time she came up from Recovery, were scentless. But *why* were they scentless? Didn't long-stemmed roses have a fragrance anymore? Had the fragrance been bred out of them, or was the world so drained? And another thing: The mosquitoes in this hospital had no sound. Toby had seen two in his wife's private room since she had been there, two in two days, and neither bug *whymmmed*.

"You're hungry?" Toby asked.

Ellen nodded, blinking and chewing.

"Well, you should be," Toby said, unsticking his long bare runner's legs from the plastic chair in the heat to stretch them full length. "Jesus, Ellen, you had another eight-pounder yesterday. Two eight-pound boys, in four years. That's a lot. Don't you remember how famished Katey Foster was after she had her two boys?"

Ellen tilted her head modestly to the window as she chewed, chin sideways. Then she swallowed, the chin up, the delicate throat taking down an amount of food so astonishingly large that Toby had to gape—she was always doing things like that, these days—and turned back with a question.

"Don't you think I'd be so hungry if I'd had girls?"

"I don't know . . ."

"It does seem, though, that it takes more out of a woman to have boys. Don't you think? For a female to produce males—it's more a stretch of the imagination . . ."

"Why do you say that, Ellen? I'm not disappointed you had another boy."

"Whoever said you were?"

"I'm just amazed! I don't know what to make of it!"

"All *right!*"

They quit looking at each other again. They looked,

together, at the fuzzy black raspberries that the tip of Ellen's fork had stopped against. The fork was moving slightly with her breathing.

"I'm sorry," Toby said, jumping up to kiss her. "I don't know what's putting me on edge. The heat, maybe."

"*Is* hot."

"Well, why the hell don't they put air conditioners in the maternity wing?" Toby exploded. He spun around to glare at the room with a baked and hopeless expression.

It was August, a heat wave too hot for clothes: Toby wore only a pair of shorts. In the late afternoon everything looked swollen and sticky: the raspberries in their fuzz coats, the roses already beginning to drip their petals, the two plastic cups of ginger ale, sweating like crazy. Toby picked up one of the cups and brought it to his lips, warm and fizzly. A drop fell to his thigh, where there was a mark that his four-year-old son had made that morning: a bite mark. The four-year-old was not sure about this new addition to their family. Tomorrow, or the day after tomorrow, he would befriend the baby, he would spend hours singing to it and in general being an angel, but today . . . today he had bit his father in the thigh.

Toby understood.

And not only hot: It was crowded beyond belief. Heat waves brought out the babies, the hardened nurses of the night shift said. There were too many patients for the porters to clean up after. The Sunday papers from yesterday still sprawled on the floor as though they had taken wing during the night, when no one was looking, and sometime toward dawn, hot and weary, had decided to come to the floor for a rest, wings outspread. But what the papers had thought would be a rest had turned out to be death. Death; and the indignity of people trampling on them. The night nurse, beefy, with psoriasis splotches on her arms that looked like pink elbow patches, was trampling on them now.

"It's a mess all right," the nurse said. "Wasn't anybody in here to clean this up?"

"Nope," said Toby.

"Nobody, all day?" asked the nurse.

"Nope," said Toby.

"How're we making out, honey?" she asked Ellen. "You ready for the little fella to pay a visit?"

"Can you wait just five minutes, so I can finish eating?"

"I can wait, but I may not get around to you again for an hour," the night nurse said.

"It's *that* busy?" Toby asked.

"*Him*," said the night nurse to Ellen. "What does Daddy Long Legs know about any of this?"

Just in time Toby managed to pull in his bare feet so the nurse could haul toward his wife and put a thermometer in her mouth. Ellen protested with an upraised fork, but the thermometer was rammed in with an easygoing thoroughness. The night nurse lifted Ellen's wrist so that Ellen's fork dangled, and she turned her attention to the clock on the pale-blue wall.

"What's her pulse?" Toby asked after a moment.

"It smells like a brewery in here," said the night nurse, glancing at a number of small sticky stains on the floor. "What'd you do—throw a beer blast for your frat brothers?"

"It's champagne," Toby said. "My father—"

"Sure thing," said the night nurse, and flashed her pink elbow patches as she left.

There was a thud of chair hitting wall in the semi-private room next door, and their TV came back on.

From the top of the swiveling night table Toby picked up a diagram that his father had left; the doctor explaining the world to his son again. The diagram showed a penis with a dotted line through what appeared to be an excess sleeve of skin.

"How do you spell 'relief'
[shouted the TV]
In Pasadena we spell 'relief'
R-O-L———"

"Did you say something?" Ellen mumbled, around her thermometer.

"Never mind," Toby said. He got up quietly and hugged Ellen to him through the heat.

"But did you *say* something?"

"I was thinking," Toby murmured in her ear. "I was thinking that men ought to stop feeling so aggressive. Screaming, fighting, circumcising each other . . . I don't know. I feel so aggressive. Watching that baby come out of you yesterday morning . . ." Toby closed his eyes and was swamped all over again with a vision of the top of the baby's head tunneling forth, dark and wet, like a soft billiard ball with hair.

"Yes?" Ellen gently mumbled.

"Nothing," Toby said, squeezing her gently and turning back to his chair. "I just love you both, that's all. I'm just trying to stay calm."

A lawn mower came close under their windows outside, three stories down, briefly drowning out the constant gurgling of the woman across the hall—she'd been gurgling with tears all day, for some reason—before it droned off to a distant location where Toby could hear it cough out some stones.

"Here he is," announced the night nurse, wheeling in a plastic bassinet.

59

"Ah," Ellen murmured.

"You don't think he'll catch cold?" Toby asked. "With the window open, I mean?"

The night nurse turned on her incredibly surefooted rubber soles (pink, like her psoriasis patches) and stared mutely at Toby. Then she let her chin drop forward and angled it over to Ellen, as though she and Ellen were talking about Toby, not she and Toby talking about the baby. "Body Beautiful over there," she told Ellen, taking out the thermometer and whipping it. "*He'll* catch cold before his offspring does."

Responding to a bell down the hall, the night nurse sprinted from the room.

"Good luck to you in your chosen career," Toby called after her.

Ellen looked at her husband suddenly with a compassion so explosive she had to blink back tears. "Are you worried about having two boys?" she asked.

Toby inhaled.

"Because I know what you mean, if you are," Ellen went on. "It's not going to be easy. In a lot of ways, probably, having two boys is harder than having a boy and a girl, or two girls."

"I just want to make sure there aren't too many males around the house," Toby admitted. "That I haven't screwed someone out of the picture."

Outside the door, a patient in a white robe appliquéd with faded red strawberries walked by, backed up, peered in, and walked on. She had a yellow paper napkin stuck between her doughy breasts to soak up the sweat.

"So crowded!" Toby said.

Ellen blinked at him again.

Toby became flustered. "I'm just trying to think of any families where there's *space* for two boys," he explained.

"Don't be ridiculous," Ellen said softly. "Just for starters—there's Katey Foster's two boys. They must be ten and six now, it's been so long—and by all reports they're supposed to take care of each other and really, you know, make *room* for each other."

"They are?"

"That's what I've heard."

Toby thought for a moment about the idea of Katey Foster's two boys. At the end of a moment he grabbed a pencil off the swiveling night table and tapped it excitedly against his teeth. "I thought of a name for him!" he said. "Kevin!"

"Kevin," said Ellen, trying it out and beginning to smile with pleasure at its sound.

"I like it a lot," Toby said. He put pencil to paper to see how it looked—flipping over the paper with the circumcision diagram on it—but the lead broke dotting the *i*. He hesitated.

"What's the matter? Stop being so superstitious. Write it down."

"Ah . . ."

Ellen leaned back in her pillow and sighed. It was not a sigh of annoyance, Toby knew. Its opposite, rather: She admired his intuition as something fine, if frightening—there was so much of her husband she did not understand. For his part, Toby sighed, too; so baffled was he by her purity. He put down the pencil and watched with guilty suspense as a single bead of sweat rolled slowly down from her black curls; slowly, slowly to her lip; where her tongue darted out and snagged it. He roused himself.

"Well, thank goodness for Katey Foster's two boys," he said.

"Yeah, but that's such a *hor*rible story," Ellen replied with closed eyelids.

"What is? What's horrible?"

"About the kids and everything. The way they're still in wheelchairs."

Toby knew nothing about it.

"I don't know how you haven't heard," Ellen said, opening her eyes and using the palms of her hands to push herself further up in bed, grimacing with the discomfort of her stitches, reaching over and with the back of her knuckles waving an *unrhymming* mosquito away from Toby's forehead. "You know her husband flipped out?"

"I certainly did *not* know that," Toby said. "When the hell did that happen?"

"I feel like you and I could use the time to ourselves," Ellen said. "How about if we don't spoil it talking about poor Katey."

"This must have happened after they all moved back to Boston," Toby insisted. "Is that right?"

"I guess so," Ellen said. "Yes. It was about two years ago, I guess. Her husband, the pediatrician—"

"Bruce."

"Bruce. Right." Daintily Ellen nibbled a tawny piece of roast beef she held with her fingers. "He felt he wasn't getting enough attention from his wife or something, started competing with his sons . . . I don't know. You sure you haven't heard this? I know you've been in a dreamworld, but . . ."

Ellen nibbled, then swallowed so hugely Toby could hear the squeak of meat.

"I say he flipped out; maybe *she* flipped out first, for seeing Bruce as just one more male or something . . ."

"But they were always so happy . . ."

"That's . . . yes. Remember how they put one on either side of the master bedroom, and called them stereo boys? And how they used to call it 'the house of six balls?'" Ellen glanced at Toby's eyes, which were averted. "They had everything going for them: careers, a sense of humor . . ."

At this moment the patient with the faded robe stuck her head back in the room and proceeded to whittle with some dental floss between her two front teeth. "Oh, man, did you have that corn?" she asked.

Ellen and Toby looked at each other. "No," they both answered.

"Consider yourself lucky," said the patient. She opened her mouth to show Toby and Ellen a large grayish kernel of it stuck between her two front teeth. "I can't even get this piece out," she said, and disappeared, shuffling down the hall in paper hospital slippers.

The lawn mower droned close beneath their windows like a long and boring argument; then violently shut off, surprising Toby, with the unforeseen silence, into realizing that his face was tense. He tried to relax it, as the patient across the hallway continued gurgling the soft wet gurgle of a not-quite-closed faucet.

"Go on with your story," Toby suggested.

"It's not *my* story," Ellen quickly corrected. "It's a creepy story that freaks me out. I don't know why you want me to tell it. You're not even listening to me."

"I *am* listening to you. I'm just not *looking* at you," Toby said.

Ellen pushed her hair back gracefully and lifted her chin to let the air cool her long neck. "Katey, I don't know what happened, but she couldn't stand it, she couldn't stand so much maleness around, so much masculine *need*, whatever it was—she just couldn't take it. And she ran off with a woman sculptor."

Toby shifted in his seat. He crossed his left leg—the one with the four-year-old's bite mark—over his right knee, and he began to swing it back and forth.

"She took the two boys with her, and went to stay in the sculptor's studio in St. Croix, near Frederiksted, I think. And Toby, what you've got to believe, what I can't convey right now because I don't have the energy, is how much they both loved the boys. Bruce really wanted to be the father for their sons, and he was beside himself that she'd kidnapped them away . . ."

"I believe it. Go on," Toby said, swinging his leg.

"Well, he followed them down there, but the authorities wouldn't let him see the kids. That's when he really started to unravel. One night he was half-crazed with rage, or rum, and he saw her carry the two boys out, and when he thought the place was empty, he set the studio ablaze."

"Ablaze?"

"On fire. He was only trying to scare her into coming home, he said afterward, but the fire really took off, and the terrible thing was, he had seen it wrong: The two little boys he thought he'd seen her carry out were sculptures, and the boys were actually asleep under that roof . . ."

"Asleep . . ."

"So it was a miracle they got out at all. Because someone heard them screaming and ran inside, but . . . sixty percent of their bodies, I think. I don't know. At least that's what I heard. I tried to block it out. Isn't that a *horrible* thing to happen?"

"Yes, it is," Toby said. He was rocking his leg back and forth.

"I'm sorry I was even reminded of it. Isn't that a *frighten*ing thing to happen?"

"Yes, it is," Toby said, rocking his leg back and forth.

"Aren't you glad nothing like that will ever happen to us?"

"Yes, I am," Toby said, and inhaled quickly then, inhaling the afternoon. He inhaled the heated stuffiness of the room, and the scentlessness of the wilted rose petals. He inhaled the smell of champagne lifting off the stains on the floor, and the sight of the dead newspapers, and the sight of the sweating ginger-ale cups, and the sounds of the TVs up and down the hallway. In the middle of his inhalation, the patient with the gray corn in her teeth reemerged in the doorway.

"I remembered what I wanted to tell you," the patient said, patting the back of her neck with the yellow napkin. "I'm organizing a softball team among all the women on this hallway. I've got access to a big field behind my divorce lawyer's house that we can play games in, or even tournaments. Would you like to join?"

Before Ellen could answer, the patient said, "I get to be catcher!"

And disappeared again.

Ellen looked over at Toby to smile her amusement at him. But Toby at the end of his inhalation was rocking his leg so hard, he hit the plastic bassinet with the infant lying in it—causing the infant to flinch his limbs, to turn into one tiny all-consuming flinch. Toby was on his feet in a second, hovering. "I'm sorry, Kevin!" he said, as the infant looked about, tensely unseeing. "I'm *sorry*," I'm *sorry*," I'm *sorry*," he kept saying, as the infant peered everywhere for the voice.

INTERCOURSE

Lucille was flirting with the tree man.

"I didn't mind the stump being here all these years," she was saying, standing in the backyard in her white bunny robe and white bunny slippers. "To tell the truth, I didn't even notice it as time went on. What I mean is it weren't no eyesore. And then you got to remember what a nice big tree it used to be before it went and died on us. We had another tree man come and take it down when that happened; oh, this must have been five years ago now. He wasn't very professional, in my opinion. How come he left the stump, is what I want to know. But when Patricia got home from school after he finished, she couldn't get over how bare the place looked. She give me one dirty look, as if it's my fault the tree's gotta go. Course she didn't pay any attention to it all those years it was up. Well, I guess it's just natural to get fond of things without even knowing it. They become part of you. That's human nature, right?"

"Who's Patricia?" asked the tree man, half listening.

"That's my youngest," Lucille said. "Mad as she could be, but of course fifteen minutes later she's out there sitting on the top of it with her coloring book. Shees! She was just in first grade then."

"How old's she now?"

Lucille pursed her lips as though concentrating on coming up with the answer to this question. In actual truth, however, she was trying to figure out what she was doing. Was she really doing this, *this*, at last? "Ten," she said.

The tree man was concerned with pouring a stream of thick oil all around the teeth of his chain saw from a cardboard can. He was squeezing the cardboard sides to prod forth the oil. Lucille's eyes soaked up this beautiful and immensely thirst-causing sight.

"What I said about her being the youngest wasn't entirely the whole story," Lucille said. "Patricia is only the youngest by four minutes, twenty-four seconds. Theresa was born first. That's how come she got the bakery named after her. Theresa's Bakery. They're both at school now. They won't be home till two-forty."

The tree man stood up. "You know what?" he said pleasantly. "This here's the wrong saw?" He walked back to his truck cursing amiably. It was a raw and overcast morning. Lucille looked at how pink her skin was getting outside her white bunny robe and white bunny slippers. She looked at the white grass sticking out of the center of the stump. She thought about her pink skin, and about the white grass sticking out of the stump, and she decided yes: intercourse.

"What kind of tree do you suppose this was?" she asked upon the tree man's return.

"Willow."

"A weeping willow?"

The tree man was kneeling to his task again. This chain saw was a good deal heftier than the former, and a slow ribbon of oil gradually glistened along its nasty-looking teeth. "That's right, Mrs. Devecchio," he said.

"Do you like weeping willows?" she asked.

"They're beautiful trees," said the tree man.

Lucille smiled.

"But they stink," the tree man said. "Her wood's too soft, rain gets in, rots her out, next thing you know she's got a stench could knock a duck out of the sky. This one here's probably rotted, too. We'll find out soon enough."

Lucille didn't say anything because her feelings were more than the tiniest bit hurt. She threw a glance at the back door of her house, then looked again at the tree man. "It was a good shade tree," she blurted hoarsely.

"Oh, they got a lot of leaves all right."

Lucille waited to see if he was again going to add something rude; he did not, and she felt relieved. Bit by bit her face returned to normal, full of prettiness, tiredness, sadness, and hope.

"I liked having those leaves around all the time," she remembered. "Practically all year those pretty little leaves would be all over the yard like feathers, turning yellow and brown, landing on the barbecue, falling on your head, so on so forth."

"Leaves never hurt nobody," the tree man agreed as he straightened up in his woolen shirt, and Lucille felt so much encouraged that they were in understanding on this point that she said, "Yucatan."

"How's that?" said the tree man.

"Yucatan," Lucille repeated. "It's what those little leaves always made me think of. Not the place Yucatan: That's down in Florida somewhere. The sound Yucatan. Don't it sound just like little leaves, blowing down in a morning breeze, or afternoon for that matter?"

"Yucatan," the tree man said.

"Yeah," said Lucille, trembling with seriousness. "Now you can't force it or it won't work. You gotta relax and let it hit you."

"It's okay," said the tree man. "I got it."

Lucille was so excited about what this told her about him, about his respect for nice things and so on, that she actually gasped.

"I admire men who work outdoors in this weather," she said, fingering the neckline of her white bunny robe delicately. "More than I can tell you."

The tree man yanked the starting cord.

"It must be freezing cold at the tops of the trees in the early morning," she said.

He yanked again with a hard face.

"My husband goes to the bakery in the middle of the night," Lucille said. "He says it's not as cold in the middle of the night as it is in the early morning."

"Is that right?" asked the tree man. "Why is that, Mrs. Devecchio?"

Lucille scratched her nose with the white nail of her pinky finger. "Search me," she said, "but he don't get home till noon."

The saw burst on with crackling and a bomb of blue smoke. The tree man revved it a few times with his finger and positioned it against the side of the stump. The noise made Lucille's heart twist with fear and craving. He sliced into the stump and the shavings flew back against his shoulder. His eyes squinted but his lips were exposed in a soft pout as he worked the saw through the sapwood. Lucille wondered what, of all things, he could be thinking about. After a minute or two, he pulled the saw out, shut it off, and began to clean the teeth with his fingers.

"It don't seem fair to Patricia," he said, brushing black gunk from between the shiny blade points. "She loses out on the bakery just because she's born a couple minutes too late."

"But Patricia's got the R.V. named after her," Lucille said.

"Oh!" said the tree man, and in a minute he activated his saw and dipped it in again. From the neighboring yard a little dog that was about the size of the tree man's thigh muscle yapped and yapped, punctuating the noise of the saw, until the saw stopped again, when the little dog ran away. In the large, vibrating silence the tree man withdrew his blade from deep inside the stump and turned his dark woolly eyes onto Lucille's for the first time.

"What'd you get named after you?" he asked.

"Nothing!" said Lucille. She laughed with surprise. "Boy, is that a good question! Nothing!" she repeated, laughing again with his eyes still pressing in on hers.

The tree man grinned at Lucille and he gestured the saw toward her in a bold and wide-awake manner. "Maybe when I get finished I'll have a cup of coffee," the tree man said, "if you got any lying around."

Lucille smiled down at the stump and blushed. Her heart was thumping out of her chest. "I even got some sugar," she said.

"Beautiful," said the tree man in a low and loving voice. His eyes sparkled as they exchanged a small smile and then, their contract sealed, Lucille stood by as he yanked the saw to life again and settled it at last into the stump's heartwood. "Whew-ee!" he shouted then, in a sudden, wild voice. "It's rotten all right! Come and get it, you godforsaken ducks!" he shouted, exposing an old wad of yellow gum in his mouth. With his face averted he gouged at the core of the stump and shot pained little glances to see how far he had to go. "*Stinnnnnk!*"

Lucille was already in the house by the time it was finished, a minute later, and the tree man relaxed his shoulders and breathed with relief at the air that smelled normal again. He half chewed on his gum and half hummed a quiet tune as he knocked the saw free of its rot, before laying it on the cold ground beside the stump. Then he leaned over and lifted the entire stump—neither chewing nor humming now—and carried it in both arms to the back of his truck, where it landed with a vanquished sound. The tree man brushed the dirt off the front of his shirt as he loped to the back porch, and he gave the door a couple of solid knocks.

"Screw you!" screamed Lucille from within.

The tree man stood gazing with pure amazement at the painted wood of the door for an instant. Then he felt the gum in his mouth and he came to. Slowly he turned and walked back across the yard to his truck, reaching down and grasping the chain saw without breaking his stride. He tossed the saw onto the passenger seat, and he hoisted himself in, and he sat there in the cold driver's seat for a full two minutes, shaking his head. Then he got out of the truck and he went around to the back porch of the house again, and he spoke through the door. "I apologize for my brutishness," he said, and presently the door swung open, and he swallowed his gum, and ducked his head, and stepped into a place as splendid as any place in the Yucatan, wherever that is.

INSIDE THE VIOLET

(for Marjolijn Wijsenbeek)

Grady Vandergiesin was in the third-floor cubicle of his
office at the Art Museum, practice-tying his bow tie, when
the thunderstorm struck. *Bang!* Out of the blue! For twenty
minutes he'd been on tiptoes, smiling with concentration
in the mirror as he tied and untied the laces of his bow tie,
avoiding again and again, with conscious decisions each
time, the stack of university monographs to be correlated
on his desk. "Van Gogh's Nature Studies: *The Hay Stack* as
Metaphor." "Van Gogh's *Potato Eaters,* and the Raging Appetite of Art." Grad'y own private work, a critical study as
large in outline as Van Gogh's *Potato Eaters,* was going too
slowly to be good. It was too un-raging. The bow tie was
an anniversary gift from his Eloise. ("To get to be an assistant curator at Peabody," she had said this morning,

holding the two ends high like a ribbon of valor or a polka-dotted noose, "you've got to *look* like an assistant curator at Peabody.") Grady was as skinny as an average fourteen-year-old girl. Both he and his wife recognized that older men, older curators, would always be eager to take him under their wings, because he was delicate. Both of them recognized that Grady should encourage them to take him under their wings, because it was politic. Just before the first thunderclap hit, Grady was on tiptoes in the mirror, smiling like a bride. Just after it hit, he was like a diver on a high board that has suddenly begun shaking in an earthquake: crouching, white-faced.

"Goodness . . ."

It was unbelievable that such a thunderclap could come so without warning, in the middle of a calm summer afternoon. Grady crept to the window, his path as precarious as a rattling diving board. Gripping the knot of his bow tie with the soft fingers of one hand, he held on to the plastic shade with the other as it rose cautiously upon a purple world. Grady breathed. That his entire window should contain a full length of purple thunderstorm was something he had never considered before. But there it was, becoming deeper as he watched, as though a huge malevolent violet, a fabulous flower of evil, were swallowing up the bright afternoon, the campus, the sounds of laughter . . . He felt threatened, his lips pursing in and out with concentration; he felt stirred. He let go of his bow tie to open the window and cautiously he put out one palm, the bulky raindrops missing it at first, then in the next seconds splattering it, pelting it, shaking it. "My gracious," he uttered, pulling back his hand in alarm and slamming shut the window, "not raindrops but . . . water bombs." One of the big-boned curators with tenure was bumping his way down the corridor outside Grady's door, discoursing expansively to a student. ". . . Changes the ions, don't you know," the curator was intoning. "Some painters I've examined claim they do their finest work when it storms!" The curator's deep laughter became muffled as he stepped into the lavatory, which was adjacent Grady's office. Grady remembered that his Honda was exposed.

On the stairs Grady knew he was going slightly fast. His hand was leaving a watery streak down the polished oak banister. He forced himself to contain his excitement, but halfway down, there was another thunderclap—*bang!* a second time—and he leapt to the second-floor landing. He took the final steps gracefully but at high speed; like a lover, he thought wildly, in a ballet. He was flushed on the first floor as he tried to get the Museum's secretary's attention.

"Miss Scott," he said, "ah, ah, Miss Scott." She had her back to him, typing dictation off an earphone. Grady had a crush on her, which made him shy—on her shoulders, specifically, which moved like baby birds under her flimsy shirts, and on her bras, which were always black. He leaned into the space over the bottom half of her door, and rang a bunch of hangers.

A turn.

"Did I startle you?"

"No."

"My Honda," Grady said. "It's getting wet."

They giggled together.

"What will you do?"

"Bring it home, I guess," Grady said. He stood there looking at the earphone cord coiled around the dark breast of her shirt. Then, nodding to himself as he turned, he flapped out the leaded doors and down the steps into the storm, bow-tie laces flailing.

The wind was remarkable. It filled the windscreen like a mainsail, nearly rocking the Honda off its kickstand. Grady's tan cashmere jacket, a gift from his father-in-law, was turning dark brown with the rain as he bent with his full weight to close the side compartment, his mouth kissing the vinyl— but the snaps would not click. He left the side compartment open. He climbed onto his seat and activated the Honda, revving it in neutral. It was disturbing, like a physical memory of grade school, to have a wet top and bottom in the middle of the day. He revved the Honda deeply, then drove an erratic course through the parking lot, not paying attention as he fumbled for the foot rests. The rain drenched bangs of his lank hair into his eyes. "Ho!" he shouted, barely missing the Museum chairman's black-and-gray Cadillac.

The afternoon had turned to night. As Grady puttered past the campus green, the sky cracked open with two lines of light, producing an impression (which took an instant to develop) of students scampering like ants in all directions. The next impression, developing a shutter-click after another lightning crack, revealed hundreds of wild orange tiger lilies on a wet rise behind a black fence. Next was bosoms, the world loaded with bosoms wet and straining against shirt fronts, and distinctly of two types: either heavy as slumbering chickens inside sweatshirts, or skittish as rabbits behind silken blouses. Then the sky seemed to lighten again, or Grady's eyes adjusted, and everything was gray and fluid as water. An overweight girl was standing in a puddle, swatting her broken umbrella against a tree trunk. A running boy seemed to be slapping at his dripping beard as he ran. Only one person did not seem to be in panic. Was that Grady himself?

He would take the highway home, but not for a minute. First there was a cleaning lady to be witnessed standing on a second-floor balcony with her hand to her throat. There was a bird with a black worm in its yellow beak streaking past the windscreen; Grady had never seen a bird so close in flight. The side streets were paved an inch thick with

green leaves. And the perfume of plantlife everywhere!—
wet and swollen and lustful. Grady wondered for the first
time why he had purchased a Honda: that look back there
on the cleaning lady's face; sitting down so low in the rain,
he had appeared to her a child. Why not a Harley, to
scare the daylights out of the Art Museum! Suddenly he
hated the Museum. He was scooting past it again, faces of
his colleagues pressed against the inside windows like little
spider heads. They were self-important people, he knew
suddenly. Fearful, too, examining life through fogged-up
magnifying glasses without taking the plunge themselves.
Three or four of the wives, Grady knew for a fact, were so
stingy they collected Lord and Taylor boxes to put their
K-Mart gifts in. And the men! Pretending to be unim-
pressed by the famous painters to whom they were intro-
duced, acting critically aloof, then later boasting about all
the drinks they'd shared. Grady cackled, slimy with excitement. He felt himself to be slipping deeper, more lus-
trously, inside the violet. Brotherly sparks of lightning
were going off beside him left and right, illuminating his
progress. He was one with the erotic perfume of plantlife!
Around the corner from the Museum a tree was down, one
of its largest limbs sticking straight out into the roadway
and alarming Grady. Swallowing hard, he got over his
alarm. He jumped off the Honda and wrenched back on
the limb until, with a huge watery snap, it broke for all
time to a strength greater than its own. A Japanese girl
dancing under a watery downspout across the road cupped
her mouth to shout through the wind: "You did it! I didn't
think you were going to be able to do it!"

———◇———

Always before he had been afraid of these girls, these
beautiful girls on the street, the dancing girls, the girls
with violet-colored fingernails in waterspouts; they seemed

a labor union of beauty, with prejudices and privileges that specifically excluded him; but from his sudden vantage inside the thunderstorm Grady realized they were not unionized, they were not All Women, global and timeless; each was only herself—laughing as rain streamed down her face.

"Get in!" Grady shouted.

Across the road she moved her mouth, a pout that was a smirk for him alone. She seemed ready to understand. "I can drive you!" he shouted, indicating the side compartment. He was stopped in a river; she laughed, forging it on tiptoes.

Instinct started him off again, steering him through the rain the way a bird is steered. He took a corner too fast; the saddle bag popped open, extruding maps, extruding a cap gun. His daughter's. With the Japanese girl's bold laughing eyes slightly below his in the side compartment, Grady held the gun in his hand, marveling at the grime it gave off, the smudges. He fired. *"Bang!"* It wasn't loud enough. He aimed the cap gun at his ear as he drove, with the girl's painted lips laughing, her fragrance like purple flowers. *"Bang!"* at his ear. *"Bang!"* In three bangs his head was filled with thunderstorm. He was just as loud as it.

"Where to?" he asked.

"The dorm for married students; turn left."

He darted through rainy streets. It had gotten cold. The girl shook her rich black hair, laughing. The hot rain was slanting like ice onto his lap. He liked having a flooded lap now. He liked the lightning. The fragrance of purple flowers filled the side of his face nearest the girl, and when he turned to take off his darkened cashmere jacket and stuff it around her shoulders, it filled the front of his face, too. "You're only one girl," he shouted.

"And melting before your eyes," she laughed, stuttering with the cold.

"What are you going to do at home?"

"After you finish rescuing me?"

"Yeah yeah," he said, his teeth chattering. He took the cap gun and fired across her at another tree broken in the storm. She looked at him. She burst out laughing again, turning red as the rain seemed to offer protection for the boldness of her words. "Thunderstorms make me horny," she said. "I'm going home to masturbate."

Grady trusted her. He trusted himself. "What about your husband?" he asked, but just then the thunder crashed again. He fired his daughter's cap gun. "Don't answer that one," he said, turning red himself a bit through his dripping face. "*How* are you going to masturbate?"

"Are you an artist?"

He turned a little more red. "Why?" he asked.

"Why are you driving around like this?"

"I'm an artist," he decided, astounded at the sound of it. He thought for a minute about this lie, which no longer seemed a lie, just for the magic of his having uttered it. How purple his life seemed, suddenly; not at all the pale flesh-colored thing he usually assumed it to be. It was deep purple now, and it had always been deep purple. Or, if not, it so easily could be! His criticism, his studiousness, even his detested diminutiveness was purple darker than he had ever given himself credit for. His steadfastness, his sobriety, not least of all his marriage to Eloise was a deep-violet flower, sometimes traplike in its intensity, to be locked so far inside; sometimes so drenched with drunk color that everything was possible, nothing was proscribed.

"I *am* an artist, and a husband," he proclaimed. "My anniversary today!"

The Japanese girl looked happy. "By making my right arm go to sleep," she shouted. "I wait for it to go to sleep, and then I touch myself, and it feels like someone else is touching me."

He ravished her. There, behind the Slavic Language Department, under the overhang of the Computer Science Department, with the rain coming down so hard that no one in the passing cars could make out what they were doing, he wolfed down her violet-colored lips, he polished off her flower-scented breasts, he squished his fingers into the filling of her that felt like mounds of wet pollen—and she was about to come. *He* was about to come, the lightning draped across the sky east and west. "That's enough!" Grady said—"we don't want to electrocute ourselves"—and they steamed, cackling laughter in each other's ears. Grady backed out from behind the Slavic Language Department, under the overhang of the Computer Science Department, and dropped her off, more sweet-smelling than ever, on the wet white pebbles in front of her dorm. The rain was still streaming down her face.

"May I keep this?" she asked, pointing to the cap gun.

"No."

"May I keep this?" she asked, reaching across and pulling at his bow tie so she had all of it, both magical ends, in her hand.

"Yes."

"Thank you very much."

"Thank *you* very much."

They laughed. He was driving home—home, in front of the storm. The rain stopped as he sped. He was outracing the storm, getting out from inside. Grady cackled to himself at this private joke: the world out here still dry, not knowing what was in store! Above the highway to the east the sky was not yet fully dark; at his exit, the sky was just beginning to turn purple—it was as though he were traveling backward in time. He puttered cackling down the avenues, pumping with his upper body to hasten the moment that he would reach King Arthur Circle. The smell of wet tar was just rising from the thin suburban streets, to mix with the perfume of swelling plantlife in anticipation of the storm. The streets were blackening with moisture, but beneath the baby maple trees they were gray, and streaked with vagrant tire tracks. An old Labrador sauntering along the middle of Merlin Drive was panting, breathing with its tongue. "You'll cool off in a minute," cackled Grady, the fortune-teller; then blew his horn, to teach it to stay off the street. Leaves were just beginning to show their milky undersides in the quickening breeze, like the panties of the little girls who would soon be running wildly about. Roofs were beginning to sweat and darken as he passed, roofs under which, he knew, acts of madness would momentarily occur. Grown men would light fires in kitchen sinks, grown women would scribble up their legs with red magic markers, and all of it would signal them as being alive. Alive, and not one molecule dead! Skidding up the driveway, Grady flapped into his house. Eloise shrieked to see him so worked up. The wind was just beginning to drive rain through the screens of the north side as he went about, valorously banging down windows. He had to jump over his daughter, who clapped her hands, saying "Daddy brought home a storm!" And for just one minute, for just one minute in time, Grady was able to pick them both up and whirl them around the room and keep them in motion for what seemed like forever.

TASTING LEAVES

Wednesday the first: Bashfully we gather in the parking lot of the nature preserve, seven, nine, twelve of us. Antisocial naturelovers all, we need the presence of an even more antisocial guide to bring us together, to stop the toes of our hiking boots from digging bashfully in the dust. When she comes—her name is Miss Heinricker, I think, and she lets the black flies flit through her rugged red hair—I can tell she harbors an instant suspicion of me. She thinks I'm not serious about leaf-tasting. She thinks I just want to pick up some serious leaf-tasting clubwoman. This is a grievous suspicion to harbor of a seriously married man, but I'm willing to let it pass if it will help bring the group together.

To show how untrue it is, though. I bought a book two summers ago on what leaves are good to taste and what leaves should not be tasted under any condition—most things with milky saps are poisonous. As a matter of fact, until Miss Heinricker gave me that look, that What-Are-You-Doing-With-These-Leaf-Club-Ladies-On-A-Wednesday-Morning-When-Their-Husbands-Are-Off-Making-A-Living look, the thought had never crossed my mind. Besides, there's another male, an old guy on crutches. Besides, the club ladies aren't that great, nor am I that great, so we make a nice ordinary everyday antisocial leaf-tasting group; let's forget the sex.

Things we will need: a hand lens between five and ten power. Jackknife. Notebook if we want. We're not out five minutes before the least attractive leaf-taster among us stands before a yellow birch tree, whose leaves smell enticingly of wintergreen, and asks me if I want to use her hand lens, which I do—but it's not detachable from the cord around her thick, glistening neck.

Wednesday the second: Trudging along, through the bug clouds, trying to wake up, trying to recall a dream where there were: tent caterpillars all over me? nesting between my fingers? when I find that I have stepped on the back of Miss Heinricker's red sneaker. We share a scowl, and that night, with my friend the bar owner Butterman over, he asks me how I can fall in love; what exactly do I know about the woman?

And on the spot I write a poem. Butterman has never seen me write a poem before, even though he was my roommate for two years in college, and he thinks my wont to do so is one giant misadventure. Also he is extremely skeptical that Sir John Suckling or Richard Lovelace could have written their poems on IBM PC's with nearly infinite RAM capability. But there, on my IBM right before his

eyes, to answer his questions I write what's in my twentieth-century heart:

BLACK FLIES

*my love trudges through the bug clouds
on our leaf-tasting treks,*

*my love always encouraging questions
about plant reproduction:*

pistils

stamens

*she wears a ruggedly red sweatshirt,
mid-thirtyish jeans with leather*

*lightning bolts just above and below the
back of each knee that make*

*my eyes flash, sopping-wet sneakers, pale
antisocial skin that I can*

*imagine imprinting, nice squint when
she's squinting against the*

black flies

*my love drives a badly dented pickup,
her ass is just the slightest*

*touch heavy, which thrills me, it proves
she's really self-sufficient—*

*however, would I recognize my love without
the blacks flies in between?*

Butterman says he has to get back to his bar. BA degree
in the Psychology of International Relations and he has to

get back to his bar. Makes me a fabulous gin and tonic before he goes, though.

Wednesday the third: Our nature group is coming together splendidly. Everyone chatters to everyone else, waves away each other's flies. The old guy on crutches apparently doesn't speak English, which is okay, but he can't be learning much. The unattractive woman who lent me her hand lens becomes less and less unattractive the more she talks about her son's adventures on his trail bike outside of Boise, Idaho. He has some pretty great adventures outside of Boise, Idaho, and as his mother's thick, glistening face takes on a look that could conceivably be called beautiful, I grow sad. I don't know why: human interaction. Even out here in nature people make people feel vulnerable. But the person I'm really feeling vulnerable about . . . is my love, of the slightly heavy ass and the badly dented pickup. I have had such fevered fantasies about her all week that I cannot bring myself to look her in the eye. Pistils. Stamens. I walk four paces behind, my heart a big bug bite.

Butterman says I am being foolish. You can't be nice to everybody but the one person you want to be nice to. Or maybe, he says, keep being nice to everybody and then it won't seem like such a big deal when you turn your niceness very naturally onto her. By the way, he says, smiling with expertise as he grinds a little mint from my garden into our vodkas, you're telling your wife all about this, right?

Wednesday the fourth: Life goes on at a fixed rate of speed. If one is fearful that it's going too fast, that there are only two more Wednesdays left to leave whatever sort of mark one decides one wants to leave, for instance, one has just languidly to sip a little vine water, languidly munch a little bull brier, and pop another Valium. It is not necessarily true that pistils and stamens will come flowering out of your mouth. It is not necessarily true that she will curse you for conjoining your black flies with hers. Focus on her less mystical aspects, such as the fact that her pen says HandiWipe. Concentrate on HandiWipe. Cling to Handi-Wipe. Wait till the rest of the group starts down the path with the black flies glued to their necks, and then move in on HandiWipe. Now you are moving, you are moving without thinking for the first time in weeks. You are grasping Miss Heinricker's rough-hewn elbow and looking deep into her rough-hewn eyes and saying, "Your shoelace is untied," and as she thanks you, as she bends to tie it, thanking you a second time with her breathless outdoorsy smile, you are thinking it's a lucky thing you're seriously married or things could really get dangerous now.

However, truth to tell: Things are a little bit dangerous already. For hours Wednesday night I am in a state, tossing and turning on our double bed at home with a horrible craving for ostrich fern, for buckwheat leaves, for the exotic root-beer flavor of sassafras. I want to taste. I want to taste. Nature is so various! And my guide so knowledgeable! To calm myself, I tiptoe from my wife's side and sneak down the back stairs to write another IBM poem:

WHAT I LIKE ABOUT MISS HEINRICKER

*the way she cups a run-over robin in her
hand and tells us not to be*

*sentimental because this too is natural,
then as we're concentrating*

87

on not being sentimental the way she lobs
the bird into the bushes so

it's a graceful burial—this is what
i like about miss heinricker.

also her information that certain pine cones
are so tight that only

a forest fire will release the seeds; her
information that all species

will cut themselves back after they achieve
maximum density; the way

she includes war in her view of evolution—
in a word, her long view.

she once showed me a tree that had been
sickled in its infancy, and

when it had come back it had disguised
itself; it had changed the

shape of its leaves! all these are things
i like about miss heinricker.

about the only thing i don't like is her
cluster of red fleabites.

I feel slightly better and now I go to sleep.

Wednesday the fifth: My love arrives wearing pale-purple lipstick and vibrant-green eye shadow to trudge through the bug clouds. She looks as fearful of me as I once did of her. Seeing her love so nakedly exposed, I run over immediately and brush a spider off the back of her sweatshirt. I brush a ladybug off her shoulder. We talk about this and that. She's limping. I like that. She got her limp chasing a baby squirrel forty feet up a pine tree; it jumped to a hemlock, but she caught it anyway. I like that very much. Creeping along her collar is a pale-green inchworm which I don't brush; I think that would be pushing things.

Butterman asks me do clothes have anything to do with my unlikely success? He has been jealous of my unlikely successes, once I get past the panic stage, since our sophomore year together. I say no. He says what have you been wearing? I tell him Harris tweed with horn-rims the first Wednesday, khakis and sneakers the second, dungarees and a work shirt the third, dungarees and I think a work shirt the fourth, and my pink Christian Dior shirt the fifth. The pink Christian Dior, he says, with the monogram on the pocket that looks like you've been on an all-night debauch? Yes, I say. Ho ho, he says, slamming open a newspaper, you're lucky I'm not a woman or I would *stay away.*

I look out the window at the passing hordes of moths.

Ten or fifteen seconds further into the evening Butterman slams down his paper and asks what my dreams have been like. I say nothing out of the ordinary: people spraying each other with insect repellent, et cetera; what about his? He says he has been having explicit dreams about my wife. What sort of explicit? I ask, but I can see from the expression on his well-educated bartender's face he expects pistils and stamens to flower from his mouth. We share a distinctly tension-filled, uncollegiate silence. He demands to know what the blanket is doing in the back of my Jeep. I tell him I always carry a blanket there in case I have to cover something stealable. Why? I say—you really got to tell me, I really got to know. Butterman wipes his lips. Because if you were moving off with the leaf-tasting guide, he says.

Wednesday the sixth: All week I have been in a sweat antic-
ipating Wednesday the sixth, final field trip, push coming
to shove. Miss Heinricker maybe getting a tick on her calf
and raising her trouser leg to pluck it, maybe giving me a
look when she points out the spittle certain bugs like to
play in, maybe leaving under my windshield blade an IBM
poem hot off her own twentieth-century heart. No? Yes?
Who's to say what disasters may befall two people who fall
in love tasting leaves? Yet I awaken before dawn with two
dreams.

I dream I have no choice but to break up with my love
the leaf-taster. It is absolutely silent, for she has become
some sort of plant, she is in a red flowerpot, and very
chivalrously I water her, so that the water goes down
smoothly and aromatically, and then with utmost delicacy,
I remove her from her flowerpot and transplant her, set her
free in a field of clover. Part of me wants to drop a tear as I
do this, but no tear comes.

Also I dream that I am breaking up with her at a florist
shop. This time it is noisy as I rush into the greenhouse
area where she is; however, I am not here to pick her up,
as she thinks, but to say good-bye. Surprise, hurt, anger—
she swats at me, threatening suicide on the spot. In real
life, should people ever swat at me and threaten suicide, I
would be crippled, I could not deal with it at all, but in my
dream I know exactly what to do: Immediately I take her
to a doctor, who looks like Butterman, and who sadly
hands her a certificate saying it is okay for her to kill herself. I take her to a priestess, who looks like my wife, and
who with genuine sympathy hands her a similar certificate.
My leaf-taster is all cleared for blast-off, but now suddenly
she panics. She opens her mouth and screams at me, with
words that wildly fill the air and spume everywhere like

some desperate, detoxifying gas: that men are parasites, that the world is a poisoned place. The words fail to disinfect, fail to purify either of us of our lustful sufferings. With a fullness of breath and a clarity unknown to me in my waking hours, I cup her lovely rough head in my hands and tell her no, men are not parasites, the world is not poisoned, it is not a poisoned place: This is just the way passion is.

GROWING THINGS AT
BAD LUCK POND

When the two of them had finishing planting the white crab-apple tree they went back to the screened-in porch and rocked on rockers in opposite motion and kept an eye on the tree. Then the father said, "There we go, now—a sparrow's lighted on one of the branches." In his view of things that meant it was a bona-fide tree now, something they had started that had managed to take on a life of its own, and also, therefore, that it was about time to get busy again. The son had to move his head this way and that in order to make out the brown flickering bird through the screen, his eyes weren't as good, but at last he saw it, too.

"How about that!" said the father.

"Pretty good," the son said lamely.

"*Pretty* good?" said the father. "Hell, I'd plant fifty of 'em!" This meant he thought the planting was more than pretty good.

"I just love to see things grow," he told his son with authority. "The first thing your mother and I did when we bought this place was to put in the garden. Of course, we didn't know anything about gardening then, not one thing. I remember on our way up here for our very first weekend we stopped at a hardware store in Charlottesville. Your mother waited in the car and I walked inside and I picked up a packet of corn seed and I asked the clerk, 'What does it take to raise this stuff?' and he answered, 'Just dig a little hole and drop in the seed and cover it over and make sure it gets some water and some sunlight and up it'll come.' And I said, 'Up it'll come?' and I remember it struck him, too, all of a sudden, what a miracle it was. Corn! And so simple! We both of us stood there shaking our heads in wonder."

The father inhaled deeply and trembled with the beauty of that breath.

"When was that?" inquired the son. But the father pretended not to hear, for he considered the question mundane. He liked his weekends away from his Richmond newspaper to be perfect.

The April noontime was bright; white light streaked the grass all the way down to the dirt road below the two males, red flowers lit up the shady wooded embankment that rose behind them.

"It's nice up here," the son said.

"That's what I call a good morning's work," interrupted the father. "And I thank you for your help. We can get a lot done when we work together. How's that ankle of yours?" he asked.

The son stopped rocking to lift his ankle experimentally. "It hurts," he admitted.

"The swelling seems to be down some."

"Yes, sir; now it's throbbing," said the son.

"Well, make up your mind. Do you want us to head home for a doctor or not?" the father asked.

"Not really."

"Then don't complain," said the father. "If a person is willing to stick something out, then he sticks it out."

The son postponed rocking.

"You don't stick it out and then complain the whole time."

"Um."

With a shrug the father went out of the porch and into the little kitchen of the mountain cottage. He was a practiced cook, since his wife had died young—not talented but practiced. From the shelf he took down a packet of dried mushrooms.

The clanking from the kitchen put the son in a drowsy mood. He leaned back in his rocker to rest both his legs on the leather hassock and he sighed with disgust. A sprain would take weeks to heal. It would interfere with his livelihood: Who ever heard of a public-opinion pollster who limped? His father would have to do all the driving back to Richmond and then he'd have to support him up the steps to his crummy little apartment. He cursed his ankle to hell. The air was fragrant and layered cool and warm. He dozed.

The son was soon to be a father himself. His wife, back in Richmond, had learned a couple of weeks ago that she was pregnant. That was good. That was as it should be. But in his vulnerable, dependent state, laid up with a bum ankle in the Blue Ridge Mountains of Virginia, the thought was vertiginous. The son dreamed he was falling off the ladder again. He dreamed he was falling off the mountain itself. He was holding on, but someone was prying his hands loose. Horses reared over him; black skinny cannibals danced around a fire, their teeth were spears close up. Himself a father. . . !

The son awoke to the sound of fierce, fast chopping outside, tree after tree cracking; his father was mastering the forest. A bowl of mushroom soup sat cold on the floor a few feet from the son's rocker, and near it, a sandwich. The light through the screens had changed. It was golden and sharply reproachful: late afternoon light. He limped outside to meet his father.

———◇———

The father was shaving the hairs off his face, a thing he'd done twice a day for years and years, and still the procedure was amazing to him. It was stupendous that the beard should grow up so, on and on! But shaving was also rather peculiar.

Here is why it was peculiar. The father thought when he was twenty years of age, certainly when he was twenty-five, that he knew all he needed to know about shaving his beard. But this was not the case. The father was still learning at fifty-one—a new way to apply the lather, a new place to rest his index finger for better-balanced strokes. So far so good. But the father, standing at the ancient kitchen sink of his mountain cottage with evening coming on, realized it was possible that he had already known where to place his index finger, and had forgotten—during his life he had forgotten and relearned many things. Even words. He had memorized the word "redolent" at fifteen and had had to look it up again just last week. So there were many deaths in life, many rebirths, too . . .

He came out of the kitchen and tacked toward his son

on the porch, turning on lamps a little prematurely. He stood over his son a moment, cracking his knuckles.

The son looked up. "What say we get drunk," he said. "Just the two of us."

"I'd say you're unsteady enough as it is," said the father. "How about we make a cane for you instead? There's a perfect branch I noticed out by the well."

"Ah, never mind about it," said the son.

"Why? It'd be a cinch to make."

"I'll just hop," said the son. He stifled a violent yawn. Then he looked up again and inquired, "How's the newspaper business these days?"

"Fine."

"Think the price of paper will hold steady?"

"Of course not."

"Oh. No?"

The father began cracking his knuckles again.

"The light is fading," said the son. When he saw that this, also, his father dismissed, he cocked his head and said, "Did you hear that?"

"Hear what?"

"I just heard a couple of bullfrogs in the direction of the pond."

"It's too early yet for bullfrogs," said the father. "Bullfrogs won't be out till May at least, maybe even June."

"I'm sure there was at least one bullfrog," said the son. "Come on," he said, rising unsteadily and hopping for the door. "I'll show you. We can watch the sun going down, too."

"Well," said the father dubiously. "As long as we're going, I'll get the goblets."

It was a family custom to drink water from the pond below the dirt road when the sun went down. Then, when the sunset was done, the goblets—they were manufactured by a cousin and weren't particularly gorgeous—would be thrown far out into the water, where they'd sink, a kind of homage.

The son hopped the first grassy part of the descent, but it was tiring and he had to limp when he reached the stones in the dirt road. Balanced wearily on his good foot in the middle of the road, he could see beneath them, laid out like a stained-glass window in the burning sky's reflection, Bad Luck Pond, the cleanest and coldest body of water in the region. "Hear that?" he said, panting. "Bullfrog!"

"Couldn't be a bullfrog," said the father.

The land fell off steeply now, but by careening crazily from boulder to tree trunk, the son instantly delivered himself to the water's edge.

"Looky here," he said, pulling twigs from his hair and staring. "What'd I tell you. A bullfrog."

"Well, how about that," said the father, stepping behind him. "I'll be!"

It was a tremendous dark-green bullfrog, a sensational bullfrog, positioned like a monarch with only his front feet in the water, and he wasn't daunted by the son's proximity, though he kept stock with one sage eye.

"You'll scare him off," warned the father.

"No, I won't," said the son. He dangled his bad foot in the grass against the side of the bullfrog's abdomen, but still he didn't budge.

"That's one brave bullfrog," conceded the father. He started to step next to his son but the bullfrog vanished beneath the surface of the water.

"Jesus Christ," said the son contemptuously.

"What'd I do wrong?" asked the father.

"You tried too hard."

The father thought for a moment. Then he said something in a voice that he reserved for his talented but crazy brother, for his talented but crazy sister, for pushy pan-handlers, for reporters he was forced to lay off and who were looking for someone to blame, for anyone at all who came at him with unsteadiness—a polite and measured voice. "If the world were a bullfrog, you could be king," he said, and then he took a long, appreciative sip from his goblet. The son watched him drink.

"Sun's down," said the father. He reached back and tossed his glass far into the air. After a while the son threw his glass, too, but his strength was diminished now and it was a short throw. The bullfrog hadn't returned.

"It's beautiful and it's mysterious," the father said with boldness. "You want to go back to the house?"

"I don't think so," said the son.

"Either you do or you don't," said the father.

"I don't think so," repeated the son carefully.

"That's what we like over in the publishing club," said the father. "A young man with his mind made up."

The son forgave him again with silence. The sky grew darker, with tips of the evergreens stuck to it.

"You've got a fine woman for a wife," the father said.

"Thanks."

"A real lady."

The wind rustled the dead branches on the far shore.

"What are your thoughts on becoming a father?" asked the father.

"It hasn't really sunk in yet."

"I see."

"It baffles me," said the son. "It's wondrous."

"Well, don't let your wonder slow you down."

"No, sir."

The father cleared his throat. "It's going to be a clear night," he said. "You want to go back for supper?"

"If you do."

"This is a beautiful, restful place to escape to," said the father. "But it's no place to live year 'round. It's more a place to come for a rest after working hard all week in Richmond."

The son thought about that for a minute. Then he said, "I'm not asking you for this place."

The father smiled wearily in the darkness. "But I wish I could offer it to you," he said.

"Why?"

"Because I know you love it here. And you hate living in Richmond. You hate the grind, and you hate the rat race, and you hate committing yourself, and you hate proving yourself, and you hate your job."

"Such as it is," volunteered the son.

"Such as it is," agreed the father.

The son felt he wasn't supposed to say anything more, but he took a breath and said, "Then why won't you offer me this?"

"Because I want you to make it on your own!" said the father. "I want you to stand on your own two feet and be able to look anyone in the eye and yell: 'I made it in the real world. Not in the bullfrog world. The real world!'"

When these words had settled down across the water the son said, "You want to have supper now?"

"No!" cried the father. "No, I don't, damn you!" He grabbed hold of his son's head and he squeezed it into his shoulder and he stood there hugging him like that for a long time on the shore of the pond.

The stars were showing, and the glossy moon. In the steadfast light of the moon the leafless Blue Ridge Mountains rose nude from the black water, slow and shadowless; it was like being given a glimpse of the earth's private life—the mossy felled trees, the fir saplings, the uphol-

stery of brown leaves—its at-home side, the earth in robe
and thick, ragged slippers.

And that's not all, said the earth; look around gentlemen, and see the life you're leading, it's in the moonlight revealed, your past and your future and all the lives
you'll ever lead, all luminous; how you came this far and
where you must now go, gentlemen—revealed to you like
a maze on its side.

Indeed it was like that for a minute or more before it was
over.

A slow, ghostly breeze came off the fresh water and
lifted the father's hair off his brow, and let it fall again.
Reluctantly he let go of his son's warm and tousled head.

"Let's have some supper," said the father hopelessly. In
the streaming moonlight they climbed back to the cottage
and had an early supper and said good night to each other
and turned in.

At two in the morning the son got out of bed and flew
back down to the pond. There! Was! The! Frog!

ABOUT THE SEA

"Gentlemen," Dr. Solznik said. He looked out at the banquet room half-filled with colleagues convened for the 44th annual meeting of the American Neurological Society in Chicago, at the several rows of eyeglasses tilted whitely at him under the fluorescent lights, and he smiled, and tapped the microphone, and just at the instant that he tapped the microphone, his son Brook made contact with a high-tension wire near his Dartmouth dormitory in New Hampshire, and plunged sixty-five feet to the earth, unconscious. "First let me say what a pleasure it is to see a few familiar faces amid the crush of reporters," Dr. Solznik began, sparkling a wry chuckle to spread throughout the room, the white-tinted eyeglasses to bob merrily and turn to left and right.

Two hours later, relaxing in his suite directly above the convention center, sucking with some satisfaction the maraschino cherry from his Perfect Manhattan while putting to his ear the latest seashell he had purchased for his hobby (a chambered nautilus sounding so much like the sea that Dr. Solznik understood, with a smile, how naive people could believe it *was*), the phone rang. It was the Dean of Men. "I have some extremely, ah, un*fav*orable news to tell you," the Dean said. "It concerns your son, Brook."

Dr. Solznik was able to catch the 7:18 flight out of O'Hare. He had to take a seat in smoking, but after Buffalo an agitated man in non-smoking stood up and asked if anyone in smoking would like to trade seats. Next to Dr. Solznik in his new location were a prep-school girl and her prep-school brother, who were en route to a funeral. The girl had been crying. She was telling her brother in a wet, passionate whisper that when she was eleven, she had come home so excited from a Saturday-afternoon movie that their parents had invited her to sit down and tell them about it. She had told them the whole story of *E.T.*, and when she had finished, their father had smiled at her and touched her wrist and said, "Do you realize it took you as long to tell the movie as it did for you to watch it?" The prep-school girl in the darkened cabin of the plane began to cry again, recalling their father saying this. "They must have loved us, to have sat through a whole two hours; they must have enjoyed us," she said between tears. The stewardess told Dr. Solznik to buckle his seat belt for landing.

In the confused compactness of terrestrial life at Logan, where electric organ chords were being broadcast over the distant sound of splashing fountains, a bony kid in a Boston Red Sox cap squinted down at him and said, "Dr. Solznik?"

"That's right."

"I'm Terry Norton, from the College. The Dean sent me."

"Is there a car?"

"Yes, sir."

Giants and midgets were rushing around everywhere to the sound of an organ being drowned. Under his Red Sox cap, Dr. Solznik could spy the boy's recent crew cut complete with barber nicks that resembled nothing so much as fault lines in an earthquake zone. Dr. Solznik clicked together a couple of Philippine forest shells he had in his pocket, and smiled grimly at Terry. "Let's get out of here," he instructed.

Terry had come down from Dartmouth in an odd, summery-looking vehicle.

"It's a Volkswagen Thing," Terry explained.

"Good for riding on the sand, is it?" inquired Dr. Solznik. "Beach buggy, that sort of thing?"

"That's why I got it," Terry admitted, smiling a self-conscious smile, all gums and eyeteeth, before adjusting his cap over his crew cut. "But it turns out they don't allow it on beaches."

Dr. Solznik and Terry and the Thing became one more pair of lights leaving the city, like those Dr. Solznik had watched from the air during his descent. He had been able to see cars crawling along blackened boulevards, rounding corners, their headlights shooting through the darkness ahead of them for a little way, for only a couple of hundred yards. Beyond the couple of hundred yards, there was darkness. That was worth remembering. Darkness. And beyond the sound of electric organs being drowned, silence. "Drive carefully," Dr. Solznik commanded. "Do not rush."

Just inside the New Hampshire line, toward midnight, Dr. Solznik made Terry pull in at a truck stop. Dr. Solznik bought Terry a cup of coffee and two pieces of cherry pie. "It's the best thing for a young man driving back to college in the dead of night," Dr. Solznik said.

"You know it," said Terry, squinting. He blew in his Styrofoam cup with more force than was necessary; a little coffee sloshed onto the Formica.

"Do you know why I'm going to the College?" Dr. Solznik inquired.

Terry put a paper napkin between his cup and the Formica, and it turned brown in a second. He looked at Dr. Solznik without squinting. "Yes, sir, I do," he said. "I'm tremendously sorry."

"Yes," said Dr. Solznik. "Well, just don't go falling off any high-tension towers. I'm sure your father has enough to worry about, without his son falling off high-tension towers." He clicked the shells in his pocket. "Finished?"

They drove on under a grave and stately moon, with a solitary star next to it like a beauty mark.

The Dean met them at the entrance of the hospital. He was a porky figure wearing a tie stenciled with either footballs or cheerfull, colored potatoes. "Ah, come *in*," the Dean said with the expansiveness of a party host, taking Dr. Solznik by the elbow and at the same time pumping his hand. "Brook is on the third floor. I've been assured he's getting the very finest attention possible. Two nurses are monitoring his condition and they have a buzzer which connects directly to the doctors' lounge in case there's any change. It's considered," said the Dean proudly, "one of the better college hospitals in the country."

"What is his condition?" Dr. Solznik asked.

"Unchanged, critical," said the Dean in a solemn voice—and just as suddenly resumed his mood. "We can take the staircase, or there's an elevator just down the hall. Ah, ah," he said, as if a great idea, a creative new football strategy, were occurring to him, "unless it's preferable to have a drink first. It's all set up."

"Preferable," Dr. Solznik said. "Yes, it's preferable."

"Whaddaya say there, Terry boy—want one, too?" the Dean asked, when they had reached the glasses in the corner of the empty, well-lit lobby.

"I don't know, Coach, I guess so," said Terry hopefully.

"Are you a coach as well as a dean?" Dr. Solznik inquired.

"Terry's a good man," replied the Dean. "I mean that. I really do."

"I just wish this whole accident had never taken place," said Terry.

With the bottle firmly in hand, the Dean took it upon himself to make a gesture of tragedy, despair, and worldwide hopelessness.

"Do you also consider it an 'accident'?" Dr. Solznik asked the Dean.

"Oh, no question about *that*," said the Dean with surprise. "The two students who were with Brook talked to me, they opened right up, that's how upset they were. And it did them a great deal of good, I think. I hope." Above his tie of festive tubers the Dean gazed clear-eyed at Dr. Solznik. "It was a beautiful autumn day, and they were out climbing."

"And all but one of them avoided touching the high-tension wire," Dr. Solznik pointed out.

"There should be no doubt," the Dean stressed, his innocence indefatigable, "the lad's fall was accidental."

It occurred to Dr. Solznik that the three men standing together did not, after all, *want* to be standing together. He lifted his glass to his lips and drank, concentrating on the rubber squeaking of nurses' shoes far away.

Terry was staring openmouthed at him. For several seconds he stared at Dr. Solznik with his nicks exposed, and then he asked, "Don't you consider it an accident?"

"Certainly not," answered Dr. Solznik. "Brook was trying to get my attention."

Then Dr. Solznik took the initiative in downing two more double shots of Jameson, and three drunk men piled into the elevator, Terry removing his Red Sox cap for the ride.

Terry and the Dean went to the visitors' lounge, the Dean plunking down stiffly in a cracked leather chair, squeezing his thumbs into his eyes until he saw green goalpost shapes, turning to the chair beside him and saying, "You're a good man, son."

"Thank you," said Terry.

"No, I *mean* it," the Dean said, shaking the student's knee. "Don't fall asleep."

Dr. Solznik proceeded down the hall and opened the door to his son's room, which was unattended. The nurses were on break.

"Brook," breathed Dr. Solznik.

Dr. Solznik took two steps through the subdued but shiny lighting of the hospital room.

"Brook," he said, stepping forward and gazing down upon his only son's porous face. "Ah, my God, Brook," he said.

Brook lay immobile in a super-white bed, eyes bulged, mouth agape, tubes going in and coming out of everyplace. The paralysis was thorough; Brook could not bat an eyelash. For some reason Dr. Solznik could see too clearly the scalp at the root of his son's hair, as if it had taken the brunt of the electric shock, so white and demented it looked. There could be no repair at this point, Dr. Solznik knew. And knew at the same second, as something akin to fury invaded his throat and he began pulling crisp leaf flecks from his son's hair, that he, Dr. Solznik, could go on living. He could continue to catch his airplanes and deliver his papers—and he would retain in his fingers the feel of every haircut he had given Brook as a boy. How many haircuts had there been? Thirty? Forty? He knew this head, its peculiar subtle landscape, like a nocturne he'd played on the piano as a young father, the long-ago notes half-familiar to his fingertips. Dr. Solznik's life would be diminished but it would not end.

His hand toying gently now with his son's useless left ear, bending and exploring it like a D flat mistakenly written into music he'd known for two decades, Dr. Solznik imagined all the splendid noise that had entered Brook's head during his lifetime, all the priceless conversation passing in and out, gone to waste, gone away . . . For several seconds Dr. Solznik stared in a sour frenzy at the abstract beauty of this ear, which was pink, and glazed slightly with yellow, like the inside of a shell—then he drunkenly leaned to put his own ear next to Brook's, and from inside Brook's ear he heard, with a clap of clarity astonishing enough to take his breath away, a roar like the roar of the living sea; "No!"; and he staggered from the room to stand bewildered in the hallway outside, blinking at the hospital portraits, until he decided that the roar must have been the hum of the hospital's machinery, nothing more . . . and he marched to the bathroom and scrubbed his hands, and he marched to the waiting room and woke up Terry and the Dean, and he filled their glasses again and again as he spoke powerfully on the irreversibility of certain neurological disorders, and then three reeling men held themselves stiff and quiet as they bumped open the glass doors into an early morning so cold and dark the stars stabbed down into their eyes like icicles.

———◇———

Later that morning Dr. Solznik dreamed Terry in his Red Sox cap was swimming underwater, lost and frantic, turning blue as he was losing his air.

He dreamed the Dean in his terrible tie was also lost underwater, alone, and panicking, as the last of his air was running out.

He dreamed both Terry and the Dean were breathing each other's breath, locked in an underwater embrace and transferring the same air back and forth from mouth to mouth, and in this miraculous father and son manner were making it possible for both of them to survive.

Soon again Dr. Solznik was sitting in the privacy of his offspring's room. Soon again he was listening at the cool glazed lunacy of Brook's ear. But this time he was sobbing terrible sobs as he thought: It really *was* the sea.

PART II

SMALL FAMILY
WITH ROOSTER

The baby falls asleep in Amy's arms on the ride in from the airport, and Amy asks her mother to keep her voice down, please. Mrs. Hunt gasps, cuts off the gossip, and guns the car. All the way to the Mansion she wears an expression that says she has tried to make the visit endurable but that, already, she is no longer responsible. Mark turns to watch the snowy billboards of Charlottesville, Virginia, and thinks what a span there is between Christmas and New Year's—six whole days. And it won't even be Christmas until tomorrow.

———◇———

Mr. Hunt is just backing out of the driveway in his Jaguar when Mrs. Hunt, Amy, the baby, and Mark pull up the driveway in theirs. Even with the two panes of tinted

Jaguar glass between them, Mark can tell that Mr. Hunt is bigger and angrier than ever.

———◇———

One good sign is that the Christmas tree in the vestibule seems to be prospering. It is a real live Virginia pine in a large planter of rich, black soil. Each green needle glistens. Extraordinarily white sand dollars hang from the branches. Mark drops the luggage on the floor near the tree and comes closer, on the lookout for good signs. Tiny white bulbs flash on all at once, then go out again, a one-second flash of mute joy every four dark seconds.

———◇———

Amy's brother, Vance, is dead. Mark and Amy have not been back to the Mansion since Vance died after last year's Christmas. Vance was the favorite offspring of Mr. and Mrs. Hunt, squash partner of Mark, godfather of Billy, the sleeping boy. Amy lowers Billy into his crib. Mark puts his arm around Amy and they watch the passage of dreams cross his smooth pink face. Outside, people proceed with baby steps on the sidewalks of packed snow.

———◇———

For a needed change of scenery, Mark and Amy go directly downtown to shop. Mark feels very New England in the midst of Southern ebullience. In the grocery, the nice salesboy runs to fetch their order while Mark contemplates the display jars of "Stuffed Olives!" "Spiced Grapes!" "Prepared Prunes!" "Peeled Apricots!" He also contemplates the cardboard display showing Larry Bird dunking a basketball, with space for fourteen dimes and thirty quarters under Larry's arm and, over Larry's head, the words "Fight Leukemia!" It is empty.

———◇———

The Mansion is unlike Mark and Amy's New England farmhouse, and coming here is never easy; however, it is less easy now that Vance is not present to make jokes. Dinner this first night is tense. Jokes are out of the question. It is hard to find a topic to discuss without arousing personality conflicts. After a few false starts, the topic tonight is: How many zeros are in a trillion? Mr. and Mrs. Hunt say ten. Amy says twelve. Mark ducks down the hall to the library and looks up "trillion" in the dictionary. From the library, he hears Mr. Hunt calling Amy an ignoramus. He hears Mr. Hunt berating Amy for spending four years burning down libraries instead of getting an education. The dictionary is on a stand. Mark is flipping pages fast. With his finger under the tiny light he finds "trillion" and is hurrying back to support his wife when she finally bursts into tears.

———◇———

On Christmas morning, Mark climbs the back stairs to the fourth-floor attic of the Mansion. There are between eight and ten rooms here, depending on whether you consider some to be large closets or small storage rooms. On the wall just inside the entranceway of each room is an old push-button light switch. Mark enters only the rooms in which these light switches work. The attic is very neat and orderly, but Mark is getting spooked. He is thinking about Vance, who had promised to teach him to skydive someday. Mark opens one door and reaches inside for the light switch. The place feels cold. There seems to be no switch, so he lights a match and discovers it is an empty elevator shaft.

———◇———

On the sill above the kitchen sink is a pair of golden tongs that Mark is wondering about. They're nifty-looking, but he wonders what they're for. He asks Ruby, who is wearing a paper-thin maid's uniform and has a tremendous turkey bone sticking out from between her front teeth. Ruby tells him that the tongs are used to remove toast from the toaster—they're a toast-taker-outer—and then she watches the disgust cross Mark's face. She bends over and claps her hands once, twice, and allows the turkey bone to wag in her mouth. "That's it, honey," she says. "A golden toast-taker-outer. Mrs. Hunt got it. She gets everything. She gets everything, Mrs. Hunt. Yeah. Even a golden toast-taker-outer. She believes in everything."

———◇———

Mrs. Hunt has been calling for Mark. Mark enters the stairwell and looks up to see his mother-in-law's head leaning over the banister. She is a pretty lady, but her head is flushed. "There you are," she says. "I'm looking for Mr. Hunt's electric razor. Did you borrow it this morning?" "No," says Mark. Mrs. Hunt has opened her mouth to tell him to put it back, but this reply makes her stop short and makes her head redden more.

———◇———

At the Club, the squash pro has white duck pants and a yellow cashmere sweater and very firm, very engaging blue eyes, and he shows Mark how far away he should be from the ball when he connects. To represent the ball, the pro drops on the court his well-worn calfskin wallet. Just teach me the game, thinks Mark.

———◇———

Mark hears a good expression from a drunk man at a party. The man puts a fatherly arm around Mark's waist and asks Mark if he is going to have the brown-bottle flu tomorrow. Mark asks what the brown-bottle flu is. "You know," says the man, removing his arm and giving an excellent imitation of someone chugging whiskey. Other than this, Mark does not enjoy the party.

———◇———

Mark is walking Billy around the coffee table—around and around. Mark is amazed at how primitive the boy is— that though they are holding hands, he doesn't know enough to keep from cutting his father off as they round each corner. Mark is charmed.

———◇———

It is snowing. Mrs. Hunt is gathering Mark, Amy, and Mr. Hunt to go for a toboggan ride. Mrs. Hunt is the only one who wants to go. Everyone else is weighing which is worse, to go or to stay home and be called "lazybones" all afternoon.

———◇———

Mark is contemplating the word "opulent." He notes its fat and glossy sound. He contemplates "rich." He contemplates "wealthy." He contemplates "comfortable." To him, "comfortable" sounds like the squash pro's calfskin wallet hitting the court floor, the flap of soft leather against lacquered wood.

———◇———

The toboggan is twelve feet long and loaded with jingle bells. Mr. Hunt sits in the back, because he is biggest and angriest. His legs are around his daughter, Amy, whose legs are around her mother, Mrs. Hunt, whose legs are around her son-in-law, Mark. What a way to die, thinks Mark.

———◇———

Amy runs into a childhood girlfriend at another party. Impetuously, she introduces Mark, and the three of them squeeze into the kitchen to talk over old times, and soon discover that old times are a bore. Still, Amy is trying to be pleasant and she would be sore if Mark didn't make an effort. He tells a hilarious story. Amy's friend is startled

and amused by the punch line, but her response is de-
layed—"Whey!"—because she has to exhale her smoke
first. Now Amy is homesick for the farm, too.

———◇———

Mark is exploring the attic again. He comes across four
boxes stacked one on top of the other. When he folds
back the top of the first box, he realizes it contains the
belongings of Vance. There feels to be a great deal of
loose, dusty paper inside. Mark removes with one hand a
silver baby rattle and with the other a silver rip-cord handle—both bent and tarnished. Mark is confused at seeing
a life so condensed, but what is more confusing is that the
remnants already look antiquated! In only twelve months
of sitting in the box, the remnants of his brother-in-law
look as ancient as an Egyptian pharaoh's.

———◇———

Mrs. Hunt has discovered a burst pipe in the solarium.
Big, slurpy drops of water are leaping from a hole in the
wall. Mark rescues a book on African violets and dries its
cover with his sleeve. He volunteers to call a plumber, but
Mrs. Hunt is very upset. Her head is red again. She tells
Mark that everyone knows you can't get a plumber the
week of Christmas. Mark goes to the living room to brush
up on African violets.

———◇———

At dinner, Mr. Hunt pours the wine and passes the
glasses down to Mrs. Hunt, to Amy, and to Mark. The
wine is ruddy in the candlelight. Ruby is slow with the
second course. "Honestly!" says Mrs. Hunt. Mr. Hunt can't
locate the buzzer with his foot—it seems to have disappeared under the new broadloom. Mrs. Hunt suggests he
ring for Ruby with the little bell on the sideboard. Amy
says never mind, she'll go to the kitchen and tell Ruby in
person. "No!" Mr. and Mrs. Hunt gasp, but Amy is already

through the swinging door. Mr. and Mrs. Hunt exchange a look that says Amy will never grow up.

———◇———

The Mansion is quiet in the middle of the afternoon. Everything is hushed. Mark is slumped back in the sofa of the living room. He watches Billy climb onto a large, antique rocking chair, sit in the middle of the seat, and practice covering and uncovering his eyes with his hands. Mark looks forward to the day when he can tell Billy about Vance, his godfather, about how sweet he was, and honest. Mark thinks maybe Vance is in this quiet room with them right now, appreciating his godson. He hopes so. He listens to the sound of piano keys being dusted in the next room. The sound is beautiful.

———◇———

For a needed change of scenery, Mark goes to the Club for one more squash lesson. The squash pro tells Mark to relax and be one with the ball. "Like Zen." "Like what?" "Like Zen," sighs the pro, wondering if Northerners will ever get hip.

———◇———

Everyone is crowding around the buffet table. Amy has a little hors d'oeuvre to give Mark, a surprise. "Close your eyes," she commands. Mark closes his eyes. Then he opens them and says, "I hate closing my eyes, okay?" They are both getting partied out.

———◇———

Mark comes down with a bug. Then Amy comes down with a bug. No one else gets the bug, prompting word to spread that it is nerves, brought on from living in that house. Whatever the case, the bug neutralizes two days of their visit. Mark doesn't eat for thirty-six hours, and he loses three pounds. The first food Mark tastes after thirty-six hours is the tip of a spoonful of strained pears. He is testing the pears for Billy. The touch of the food lights Mark's body and his mind, and he is irradiated with love for his small, immediate family—if only they could be home.

———◇———

Ruby is having one of her bad days. All she has done since 9 A.M. is sit on the kitchen stool and cry into her apron, saying "This poor house, this poor house since Vance went away."

———◇———

Mrs. Hunt is a nut for winter sports. She has collected everybody for one more toboggan run. But she wants her son-in-law to loosen up and have fun this time. Mrs. Hunt tosses a snowball at him to loosen him up. Amy fires one back at Mrs. Hunt. Soon a friendly snowball fight is under way. Mr. Hunt is not angry for the first time this visit as he crunches a snowball on the back of his son-in-law's neck. He gets less and less angry as he tackles Mark and rubs his face in the snow. In fact, he appears to be enjoying himself immensely. You really get to know people in a snowball fight.

———◇———

Mr. and Mrs. Hunt have gone to one more party but Mark and Amy have declined to go, for they are utterly, irrevocably, and everlastingly partied out. Besides, it is nice to have an evening to themselves. They go upstairs to read in bed, but on the landing Amy says, "Oh no," remembering that her nightgown is in the dryer downstairs. Mark is only too happy to get it, and in a minute he is waltzing up the stairs again with the clinging nightgown stuck to his chest like a dancing partner. Amy is reading about Catherine the Great and Mark is reading about dairy goats, and their feet are touching under the covers. Unexpectedly, Mrs. Hunt is back, yelling "Yoo-hoo!" as she mounts the steps two at a time. She enters the bedroom uninvited to tell them what a fantastic party it is and that they must *go*. Mark smells her perfume and the drinks she has had and—is it possible?—her mink coat. Mrs. Hunt curls up at the foot of the bed uninvited. She delivers what she believes to be a convincing argument. Mark's stomach is growling and he pointedly begins reading his book again. Mrs. Hunt is wearing a great deal of crimson lipstick, but now she is too angry to speak. She is giving off more and more odors all the time and is making the bed bounce. Mark is naked under the covers. Mrs. Hunt tells them they'll never be invited to another party in *this* town. When she leaves, they figure out how the lock works.

———◇———

Ruby is having one of her good days. She tells Mark the story of a friend of hers who got a new uniform from her employer for Christmas and here is what happened next: She finished her work and went home, and that afternoon the employer's family sat down to eat their turkey dinner and there was the uniform stuffed inside. Ruby laughs. Mark watches Ruby laugh and wiggle around the kitchen.

———◇———

Mark has many photographs of Vance, because Vance used to come north to the farmhouse all the time. Mark's favorite serious shot shows Vance holding his newborn godson on his knee, his strong fingers girdling the boy's chest. Mark's favorite nonserious shot shows Vance knee-deep in the fishpond, pretending to be a sea monster. It is hard to be sad when remembering Vance blasting three feet of pond water from his mouth. But now, on New Year's Eve, Mark learns that he is about to be given a new picture of Vance.

————◇————

The very final toboggan runs of the year are due. Mr. and Mrs. Hunt just had theirs and they landed deep inside a snowy rhododendron. Everyone is keenly aware of the potential for allegory as Mark and Amy make ready to take their turn. They push off with their hands and soon attain breakneck speed. They pass the rhododendron at twenty miles an hour; they make the first turn at thirty. Dry snow is bombarding their faces as they realize it is guaranteed to be the best run of the week. Mark puts his mouth to Amy's ear and yells, "What a marriage!"

————◇————

The new picture of Vance is being given to Mark by Mr. Hunt. Mr. Hunt has tears in his eyes as he takes Mark aside, removes the picture from a cellophane sleeve. Actually, it is an old picture of Vance, a blowup from a group high-school shot that was taken eight years earlier, when Vance still had short hair. Mark doesn't like this enlarged picture of Vance with short hair. Vance looks withdrawn. He looks granulated. His lips and his cheeks and his eyes have been touched up with paint.

————◇————

Mark refuses the picture.

————◇————

To ring out the old, ring in the new, and celebrate the last night of the visit, Mr. and Mrs. Hunt go to one party while Mark and Amy take Billy to another. Only dear and special friends have been invited here. Everyone sits on the floor of the living room, overlooking the river lights and the black hills of the city. Already Mark and Amy can feel pressures lifting, peace approaching. Someone puts on a record that Mark has been wanting to hear for three years. He writes down its name. Someone is leaving for a year in Japan and Mark writes down his address in case they should go there, too; who knows? The champagne tastes perfect with the Brie. Also the gin and also the vodka taste perfect with the Brie. Mark rocks happily among the guests and asks whether they will have the brown-bottle flu tomorrow, and he thinks how great it will be to have it at home!

Amy hears the baby crying from his portable crib in the bedroom. She touches Mark on the shoulder, and together they enter the dark and dream-filled sanctum, closing the door behind them. Amy holds the baby in her arms while Mark explains to him what is in store for them tomorrow, the minute they get home. In the barn, the reception committee will be ready. First to greet them will be the pig, the old and tired pig, who'll twitch her ear and go "Oink." Next will be the dairy goat, also old and tired, who'll raise her chin and go "Baa." But best of all will be the rooster, the fierce young rooster, who'll march about and flap his wings, going "Cocker-*doo*!" He'll jump onto his perch and go "Cocker-*doo*!" He'll crow from inside the horse stall, and from on top of the hayloft, and from the rafters overhead, until the barn will be filled with the sound of his welcome: "Cocker-*doo*! Cocker-*doo*!" A sound of yearning breaks from the sleepy boy as he listens to his father. Then the sound of applause breaks from the crowd gathered outside the door, and all three look up in shock.

PARTIES AND STORMS

Holly Dubois Trumbull had loved her husband with no great passion but with a love that was orderly and true, and she deserved better than for him to come home early one afternoon after thirty-two years and tell her he wished to marry his water-skiing instructor. Of course Holly panicked. She went blind with panic. The very morning after his announcement she heard a rumor that the storm pattern along the plains might change so that Chicago would *really* be inside the tornado belt, and for days she sensed on her skin an imminence, the swirling of wind and the darkness of destruction approaching from a middle distance; she imagined that the walls of their French tudor home in Oak Park would offer no more shelter to her than the sand walls of an ant house—and, speaking essentially, she was right. That was the awful thing. Whenever she came around to her senses and tried to tell herself things were not so bad and dangerous as they seemed, she had only to review the facts to relearn the truth: She was alone, she was unsafe, she was a fifty-four-year-old poet who'd been deserted.

When the panic passed, in twelve or fourteen weeks, Holly entered a period of outrage. She would be dozing at the club pool while friends murmured nearby with their Pappagallos up on white wicker, when suddenly she would yank off her bifocals and say, "*Who'd* you say voted against the ERA?" She reread her college Freud and noted with vehemence that it always seemed to be hysterical women, never hysterical men. Her husband closed her accounts at Carsons and Fields, where she'd had accounts since she was a child of sixteen, and she was justified in speaking angrily of the loss in dignity—but her friends considered the angry speaking a further loss in dignity, if not evidence of female hysteria, and Holly stopped going to the club. She began to make a new group of friends, people from self-help groups, mostly, people who she felt were seeking adventurous new ways of being sensitive to other people, and these friends helped her get out of the period of outrage and into a period of eagerness and optimism— even if it sometimes seemed to her old friends reckless, or trippy, or forced. Meantime the poetry stopped; "Thank God," she said, trying not to giggle apologetically—giggling apologetically was one of the things she was *definitely* trying to weed out of her new life. She learned a new laugh, a laugh that really let go. She chucked out her bifocals, taking on a pair of extra-large sunglasses which made her appear overeager—"But I *am* overeager," she'd admit, "to *enjoy* . . . and God knows I'm overdue!" She took up photography—obsessively!—rarely letting the

camera off her neck; and compiled hundreds of photos of
her new life, comparing them with the old photos and de-
ciding that the whole time she'd been with Phil she had
never smiled with her entire mouth—genuine smiling
came only after her release. It was true that she was a more
beautiful woman now than ever. She had gypsy-black hair,
a proud carriage, fine feminine ankles and wrists and fine
brave bones in her face that came to life, when she smiled,
so that her smiling face showed up as clean and fresh in a
bathing cap as it did when she was forty. And with these
firm good looks came a physical vitality that invigorated
those men whom it didn't overwhelm. She slept regularly
with a gentle thirty-four-year-old Dane from her color-
photography workshop and with a passionate sixty-
year-old Rumanian from her "Introduction to Darkroom"
workshop. She loved both men but she didn't tell them about
each other; it was her little secret and it made her feel
mischievous. This and the fact that she still went to the
beauty parlor weekly were the vanities from her old life
that she could not justify in her new life but that she held
on to just the same. "Oh, well!" she laughed . . . meno-
pause being in the air but not yet having occurred . . . and
so two years after the divorce she deluded herself that she
was again a whole woman, a woman fully mended, still a
frightened woman sometimes but a woman without re-
grets, a woman who even without the poetry was more
fulfilled than she ever would have been had she stayed
married to Phil and the club and Oak Park. Of course it
was not so—in only two years; and she hadn't really given
in to it. She thought she could control the process of loss,
that she was bigger than it; so hard was she trying to be
brave! But she had bravely taken an apartment in Lincoln
Park where she stayed when she wasn't visiting friends in
New York or Seattle or Sante Fe, and the only thing that

she truly allowed to upset her was that her grown-up son and daughter never invited her to visit either of their homes during this time. They thought she had flipped.

———◇———

There were the other invitations. One of them came from new neighbors in Lincoln Park who were her children's age: late twenties. They asked her to visit at their rented cottage far out in the Thousand Islands, thirteen hours by train from Chicago, and Holly hit upon two reasons why she really wanted to go. One reason was that thirteen hours was a long way to go by train, and she wanted to see if thirteen hours by herself without the distraction of driving would be fun, if she would have fun photographing scenery from the moving windows and trying to make it streak. The other reason was that the invitation was for only two nights, which reminded her that the boy, her host, was a moody character who knew his social limits—who knew he turned testy after thirty-six hours with company—and she respected that. She was attracted to people who, unlike herself, knew things like that about themselves. And so she went.

All day the patio phone at the rented cottage jingled with travel-progress reports from Holly. She was fine, and having an early lunch at a wild little Howard Johnson's near Union Station. She was fine in the Detroit station; her watch had speeded up and she'd thought she missed her connection; but a delightful gentleman, a retired dean from McGill Medical School, who was also traveling by himself, had shown her on his watch that there was tons of time. She was fine in the Buffalo station, but she'd just stopped in the snack bar for a dish of ice cream and she had *known* something was up with the hard-hat-type man at the next table who was shoveling down meat loaf and whitish carrots with his wife and two little daughters. She knew there was something about the man, something about how fiercely male he was, how he glared at his carrots; she'd watched him after he paid his bill, and when it was time to leave he'd turned to his wife and daughters and said, "Okay, troops." Wasn't that delightful? Ah, but wasn't it poignant, too? Love and kisses, she would be there in time for drinks.

Drinks were served in the long twilight of the northern isle—land of the solid-gold sunsets, it called itself, in the manner of all pretty resorts calling themselves pricey names, with more than a little hidden boast that the price was affordable. Holly stuck her sunglasses in her wild raven hair and stood barefoot on the patio and looked thirstily at the blue water and the orange horizon; it was one of the sights she was looking at professionally, as it were; and Jack held her white wine respectfully for her until the experience was finished. She turned back with her lovely brave smile and took the wine soundlessly, and had a sip, and held it in her mouth as she raised her chin and closed her eyes and took a long breath through her wonderful white flaring nostrils, and altogether she flattered her hosts by letting it go down as though it cost quite a bit more than $4.29.

"I am so glad to be here with you two special, special children," Holly said.

"Crazy woman," retorted Oona with an eruption of her sweet Irish laughter. "If you knew how much we love to—"

"Don't even answer me. Don't even use words," Holly said, shaking her head. She held out her hands to them and they walked over to her across the wooden patio boards and they all hugged. "Thank you, thank you," Holly said in a gritty voice, and Jack lowered his eyes, and Oona checked her wit, and both of them smiled back up at her without speaking, as she wished.

———◇———

For dinner, Jack made scallops. He broiled them on a hardwood plank and ringed the plank with mashed potatoes into which he alternated slices of tomato and lemon. It was a yellow, white, and red dish, and Holly said, "Goodness, I can't *not* get a picture of this!" And she ran downstairs to her room and came back up with an all-new waterproof, shockproof, too-terribly-expensive Japanese camera that also seemed overeager. Scarcely breathing, so great was her need to capture the moment on film, she bounced around from all angles snapping the flash, and Oona laughed in her light, lilting way, saying "Holly!" and "Smile, will you, Jack!"—but Jack was tense around cameras. Over dessert Holly asked him why that was.

"I'm a stingy person," Jack said.

"On, nonsense!" Holly said, her camera still around her neck. "You mean you don't like to give out your picture?"

"Yeah," Jack said. "I'm too regal. I'm too pompous. I'm too much of an asshole."

"He means he's not photogenic," Oona said with a wink. "Yeah?"

"Yeah," Jack said. "That, too. Unless I'm in a really great mood. Then I don't care."

"Well, get in a really great mood!" Holly said. "I'm in a really great mood. Oona's in her usual really great mood."

Jack considered for a minute. Then he said, "Oh, all right," and his face lost its darkness and became bright and kind. They were all three surprised and they had a nice laugh. Oona said, "Isn't that a miracle," and they laughed more, and then Holly touched the strap of her camera around her neck and her laugh changed from something warm into something more brittle.

"I don't know what makes me think of this," she said, "and I really oughtn't to laugh, but I heard about the most awful death last night. Well, you tell me if it's awful or not. It happened to a friend of a friend—"

"A man?" Oona knew to ask.

"An editorial writer for the *Sun-Times*, yes," Holly said. "Who had a great big rocking chair in his office, a family heirloom that he would sit in for hours to help him clarify his positions for his editorials."

"*Sounds* like the *Sun-Times*," Jack said.

"Yes," said Holly. "I really oughtn't to laugh, Jack."

"Okay," said Jack.

"Apparently he was a furious rocker," Holly said. "The harder the issue at hand, the more he'd rock. Veddy serious work, you understand. Public trust, and all that. Anyway, after one of the Supreme Court decisions they came in to get his copy, and he'd broken his neck."

"He fell over?" Oona asked.

"With his white shoes in the air," Holly said. She made a shuddering kind of laugh. "I don't know which Supreme Court decision it was."

"Maybe I shouldn't tell you about a really awful death," Jack said.

Oona touched his water glass. "Maybe you shouldn't," she said.

"Is it true?"

"Oh, it's true," Jack said. "It happened to the father of a kid I knew at school. He choked on a piece of gum during orgasm."

"Horrible!" Holly cried, grasping the camera strap around her neck. "Oh, I never thought of such a thing! And died?"

Jack nodded. "I knew another guy who had such lousy service at a restaurant that when he got outside he turned around to face the building and said, 'Never again!' when he was hit by a Trans Am. Five teenagers in the Trans Am."

"Maybe you'd better get back in a bad mood," Oona stressed.

Holly was clenching her camera strap in her fist and seemed to be concentrating on something. "There was a man in a motorboat—"

"Oh, that's an old one," Jack said. "Hit a wave and went flying out? And bumped the steering arm on the way out so the boat turned and came after him?"

"Excuse me," Holly said. Carefully she removed her camera to the tabletop and then she ran to the guest room downstairs, leaving Jack and Oona at the table with an embarrassed silence.

"She brought it up," Jack said.

"You're a flake," Oona said.

"I thought she was having a good time."

"You really *are* a flake."

"I didn't tell the best part," Jack said. "My friend's father's orgasm was self-induced."

Oona stuffed her linen napkin inside her mouth to smother her laughter.

———◇———

Holly stood in the dusty guest room downstairs adjusting her blouse evenly around the outside of her belt and holding her head steady. There was a canopied bed in the corner where she was scheduled to sleep, and its presence troubled her and made it hard for her to breathe. She could imagine lying there, between the gauzy curtains, with a sleeping pill in her that would not make her sleep but would make her feel paralyzed. She imagined lying paralyzed during a windless night, stuck with her view of the underside of the canopy, and hearing the insects outside, and hearing the children crashing around upstairs in their lovemaking, and being too unhappy *to record anything on film*. Horrid. Then Holly spread a drop of Poison along the top of her left collarbone, and smiled a dazzling brave smile into the mirror, and walked upstairs to the kitchen, where they were washing the dishes.

"I'm ready to party," Holly announced.

Jack and Oona were surprised, but Jack said, "'Party' is not ordinarily used as an infinitive."

"I'm talking about a *wild* party!" Holly said.

"Hm-*bm*!" Jack said. "But I'm beat. It's twenty past nine. Aren't you beat?"

"It's supposed to storm," Oona said. "That's another infinitive."

"Really a storm?" Holly asked. "Do you have any cats around this house?"

"Why?" Oona asked.

"You *do*?" asked Holly.

"No, we don't," Oona said. "Why?"

"Well, you don't want them near you during a storm. It's an old legend of some sort that their eyes attract lightning. I mean they pull the lightning down and then they flash it onto *you*."

Elegantly, Jack picked an eyelash off his tongue. "I could go for a party," he said.

Shortly after that the living room had twenty people in it. A couple of the men were wearing raspberry-sherbet trousers and Gucci loafers with no socks, a couple of the women were wearing pumps and patchwork madras skirts with freckled legs, but most everyone else didn't look like resorters. A lot of mouths were open with laughter, but it wasn't too loud. Someone was talking about what a compulsive worker he, himself, was; that whenever he tried to take off an afternoon he would feel so guilty he would walk in his sleep to the stairs and fall down them. A woman who was standing with her back to the man who'd said that turned around and said, "Oh, did that happen to you? I once fell *up* the stairs and twisted my ankle." Across the room a woman was telling another woman who didn't look pregnant not to worry about labor, and a third woman agreed by saying it was nothing compared to the raising of kids. "When it gets really bad," she said, "I lock myself in my study and bite the phone book." That got a laugh, but the woman kept saying, "I mean it, that's what I do." A man who was flirting with Holly boasted that the cottage he was renting had a bidet in the master bathroom, but Holly could tell he immediately regretted telling her that, immediately questioned whether it was something to boast about. To get out of it, the man said that his ten-year-old son had seen it and thought it was a broken toilet. He repeated his son's words. "It's a broken toilet!" he said, and then the man chuckled and reddened and kept chuckling and reddening. Outside, the wind was picking up. The patio lanterns were swaying, and they made Holly feel like swaying, too. "Why not?" she said, consciously beating down her inhibitions—and started to sway, less like a lantern than a piece of seaweed floating on the ocean surface, shuffling in her bare feet, and holding aloft her Scotch with a hand that she purposefully kept as limp as possible. Then she remembered something; she put down her drink and jumped through the room and scooped up her camera and resumed dancing her trancelike dance, shuffling slowly toward her various targets, slowly, slowly, then: *snap!* with the camera, and off she'd shuffle some more. It was startling, the flashes of light against the dark party, and one of the sherbet-colored guests waltzed up to Jack and said, "What does she: need some instant memories or something?"

Jack grinned icily at the impertinence. "She's a lovely, dignified woman who's having rough times," he said.

"Wow, *divorce*," said the guest, waltzing away. Jack got

irritated and walked into the kitchen and popped a cherry tomato into his mouth, took another one, rinsed it under the faucet, and popped that one, too. Oona came in with a Fudgesicle.

"What do you think?" Oona asked.

The lady who bit phone books walked in.

"I think we've got another field mouse," Jack said. "I saw it scurrying along the wall near the tape deck."

"Really?" asked the lady, wide-eyed.

"It was like it was on wheels," Jack said. "It was brown. It was cute. I want to get a mousetrap and break its skull. Is what I think," Jack said.

Oona gave the lady her Fudgesicle. "Jack's getting in a mood," she told her.

Holly came rushing in, at the point of tears. "Take hands," she said.

"Did someone insult you?" Jack asked.

"I just got sad," Holly said. *"Take hands."*

Jack and Oona each took one of her hands. Holly held on tightly and tried not to cry, then she pressed a hot young hand to each eye and couldn't help it. "It's nothing, it's nothing," she said very quietly. Someone tried to come into the kitchen, but the lady who bit phone books gestured no. "I just want a broom," the person whispered, and the lady looked for one but couldn't find one. Finally Oona said, "Broom closet," and the problem became solved. Holly took the two young hands away from her eyes and smiled—wet, brave, and dainty. She looked extraordinarily beautiful, her eyelashes wet like that, and her camera was wet, too.

"Do you want me to chase these clowns out of here?" Jack asked her.

Holly's smile turned down at the corners and she quickly shook her gypsy head no.

"Would you like to stroll on the patio?" Oona asked.

"Or on the beach?" asked the lady who bit phone books.

"It's going to storm too heavily for the beach," Jack pointed out.

"Oh, I've even got a nylon jacket for the beach!" Holly said. "Oh, Jack," she begged, "wouldn't it be glorious to photograph a storm this time of night—the wind and the surf?"

"Absolutely not," said Jack. "We'd get hit by lightning."

"There's no lightning," said the lady who bit phone books. "It's not even raining yet."

Jack grinned at her.

"Don't let me prod you into anything," Holly said. "God, isn't it marvelous to be eighteen again?"

———◇———

The dunes were like great cool pools of cream to the soles of their two pairs of feet. Holly was explaining with great objectivity how she sometimes got sad, with no warning, how she sometimes got fearless, and could do anything, but then at other times how she got too scared to walk into a store and buy a toothbrush. Holly was holding the camera with two hands, periodically flashing it to light up the path, as she walked in front of Jack, who was picking his way behind through the sharp dune grass. The cold sand was swirling at their ankles and getting into the cuffs they'd rolled up as the party sounds blew off in the wind.

"And another thing," Holly said. "Did you ever feel so restless that you felt you had to do something new! Entirely new! That you had to do something entirely new or you would go crazy! Or perhaps that's putting it badly."

"No, I understand that," Jack said.

"It's not necessarily"—*snap!* in the dark night—"a *bad* feeling," Holly said.

"Try to keep the flash pointing in front of us," Jack said.

"In a way it's a good feeling," Holly said. "It can keep you young, I think. It can stave off death, I think. It makes you want to live recklessly!" *Snap!* "It makes you want to be"—*snap!*—"bold!"

Jack reached forward and put his hands on the back of Holly's waist and trained her straight ahead. They walked in single-file silence for a minute. Then they reached the crest of the beach and the wind nearly knocked them over. The air inside their lungs became humble before such a wind and they had to gasp to get their breath. "Oh!" shouted Holly. "Are those sea gulls?"

"No!" shouted Jack. "Whitecaps!"

Their clothes flapped about almost painfully. Holly turned her back to the wind and flew—sailed—diagonally to the water and waded in up to her knees. Jack followed and stood so their elbows were touching. The water was rough and mysteriously warm.

"Give me your camera," Jack shouted.

"Can't I keep it?"

"You might lose it. Don't you feel how strong the current is?"

Indeed, the current was wicked; it was groping like thousands of liquid hands. But Holly smiled and indicated the waterproof kangaroo pouch on the front of her nylon jacket. "I can keep it here and it won't even get wet," she yelled back, and she tucked the camera inside and zipped it up and began to skip about in the black water. It was like a child's dance, all joy and freedom and very little thought, and it made Jack feel old and stiff as he walked along beside her, in case she fell. Jack got more embarrassed as she clapped and sang and pranced like a Hare Krishna person, practically. Then she did fall, but it made her laugh, and she sat in the water very happy, accepting

137

the three tiers of waves as they came rolling in to her chest. Jack stood in attendance close by, but he avoided looking directly at her. He was a little scared of her, of what kind of lightning he might find flashing from those eyes in the darkness. He was also a little put out. He planted his feet in the sand to steady himself against the waves and he watched his cottage in the dunes, its windows lit with colorful clothes; people leaving, arriving—

Suddenly Holly shrieked. Jack lunged for her but Holly shouted, "My camera!"

Jack straightened back up but Holly was splashing the water frantically with her hands and feet. "You don't understand!" she shouted. "My camera! No, no! It's gone!"

Jack walked about in a circle hoping to stumble across it but he was annoyed by her frenzy and Holly soon sensed it. Evenly, though with a slightly dazzled voice, she tried to explain this: that she had had it with her, and then it was gone.

"I know that," Jack said. "You don't have to explain it."

"I'm just amazed," Holly murmured. She stood up in the water and put both her dripping hands on her hair. "I just never—it's just totally baffling to me. How could it have gotten out of the zipper? How did the waves rip it open?"

"You can fix the pouch in the morning," Jack said. Not nicely he added, "You can stitch it so it stays closed."

"Yes," Holly murmured. "Of course I can."

"We'd better get back," Jack said.

"Yes," Holly murmured. She started to wade to the shore but there was a flash of lightning—*snap!*—and she froze. "Are you all right?" Jack asked, and Holly looked at him in a dazed way. "The gods took my camera," she said, with an attempt at a smile, and she held on to his arm on the dark and drizzling walk back. It began to lightning more—*snap!* across the sky!—and when they reached the patio Holly stood about nervously, making a little crying hum like a child in nursery school, and poking her hands in and out of her busted kangaroo pouch. "I think I want to go to bed," she said.

"That's fine," Jack said.

"I think I don't want to see anyone," she said.

They both seemed frozen by the storm for a moment.

"I'll go clear these people out," said Jack finally, and he went in and cleared them out and in a few moments he and Oona came back outside to fetch her where she stood dazzled by the lightning, humming her nervous childlike cry and shivering. "Come," they said, taking her by the hand and walking her—coaxing her—inside at last and down to her room. "I'm very tired," Holly said then. "Good night, Jack."

"Good night?" asked Jack, and then: "Good night, sleep safe." He went upstairs to close the windows against the increasing strain of the storm while Oona helped Holly out of her pants and nylon jacket and into a flannel nightgown.

"I have to learn to drink a little less," Holly said.

"Yes—and then you can teach the rest of us," Oona said, toweling the rain from Holly's hair.

"Just a little less," Holly said. "That was something I never had to worry about before. Because I never used to drink."

"Yes," Oona said, brushing the sand off Holly's calves.

"Now I have to learn it."

There was a double-snap of lightning, which for a breathless instant lit the room to daylight.

"I lost my camera," Holly said. "Did Jack tell you?"

"That's not the end of the American way of life," Oona said, with her quick kindness of a smile. "Or is it?"

Holly looked at her with the expression of a terrified

child. "You don't think there are mosquitoes in here, do you?" she asked. "I'm very frightened of mosquitoes. I stay up all night. I don't want them taking anything from me without asking," she said.

Oona took note of Holly's expression. "No mosquitoes," she said.

"It's like Jack not wanting to give away his picture," Holly said, her voice rising. "I don't want to give away *my blood!*"

Right away Oona climbed onto the sheets of the canopied bed. She put her arms around Holly so that their breasts were touching through their shirt fronts, and she rocked her back and forth. "You have such wonderful breasts," Oona told the older woman softly, "so much rounder and more wonderful than my own. Did they become bigger when you had a baby?"

The older woman pursed her lips as tears came wiggling down her face. "Um-hum," she said.

"That truly happens?" Oona asked. "Could mine become as wonderful as yours, if I became a mother?"

The older woman shook her head yes. "Um-hum," she said.

"With the first pregnancy, or does it take another?" Oona asked.

The older woman took hold of the younger woman's neck and buried her eyes in the hot young skin. "Mine got bigger with each!" she sputtered—a child's quiet sputter, and a child's quiet release, the tears streaming down onto both their shirt fronts, soaking them, until very faintly the older woman drew back to her pillow, and faintly smiled, closing her eyes as if she meant to fall asleep like that, in all those tears. Oona took a corner of the bedsheet and dabbed her tears from around the older woman's mouth, eyes, hairline—and kissed her there, at the moist hairline.

Oona closed the door and Holly was left between the curtains to witness the storm leaping closer. The thunder banged away, and even with closed eyes Holly could see the lightning become so continuous that the night was not black at all but white—crackling shades of white that seemed to electrify the rain and to reach right down inside the world and pull out its middle. For a long while the storm raged, and Holly with pounding heart listened to sounds the world was making that she had never heard in her life: the bells in the wind, the walls creaking full of water, the windows lurching at the stars; and opened her eyes at last to watch in awe what use the gods could make of her camera—snapping and snapping and putting her in her place, minuscule popper of bulbs that she was! Snapping and snapping and showing her how to light up the world: Here's illumination for you! Snapping and snapping with such blinding force that the final bit of Holly's little brave pride cracked and fell away and left off at last. "Take me," she breathed out then, to the gods—"I don't know where!"

———◇———

That was the first night. The second night of the visit began the real period of loss, where no photos are permitted.

JUMPING FROM HIGH PLACES

A phone is ringing in Philip's sleep. Ringing and ringing as Philip gropes to the surface of his sleep, thrusts a hand out from his blankets to the phone. Even as he gropes he formulates this fervent wish: that it is not the Lottery Commission, telling him he has won another lottery. Philip has had only three hours' sleep and he could not face winning another lottery. In the instant before picking up the phone he decides he will hang up if he has won. But of course it is not the Lottery Commission. It is the dial tone. It is nothing but his conscience, of course.

———◇———

Philip's wife Lynn is mad at him. She is mad that he stayed out till four-fifteen last night. She is mad that when he came home at four-fifteen, he snored. However, Philip always snores when he is stewed. It is not his fault. And he always stays out stewing over rum zombies till all hours when he needs to let off steam. It is not Philip's fault that his environmental sculptures are going so poorly that he needs to let off steam. He takes long showers, half-hour showers that use up all the hot water, because it takes him a long time to reestablish a sense of romance with the world. Is it his fault that he takes a long time to reestablish a sense of romance with the world? Nevertheless, Philip respects the fact that Lynn is mad.

———◇———

Not everything is simple, Philip remembers. Just last night Margy, his sort-of mistress, threw her rum zombie across the room because he will never sleep with her. He will only sort-of sleep with her. "Your guilt is driving me up the wall," Margy wailed. "You're so goddamn chicken. I hate how chicken you are. I *hate* you! I *love* you! You can do no wrong. You can torture me to death and I'll still love you. My love is driving me up the wall."

———◇———

Love is not simple, Philip knows. The whole business of one person loving another person is illogical. The whole business of keeping a mistress but restricting yourself to giving her back rubs is illogical. Actually, Philip knows, environmental art is illogical, too—but Philip doesn't want to think about environmental art. He doesn't want to think about what a chicken of an environmental sculptor he is being these days. He wants to clear his head of all environmental art and just have a nice, suburban shower— yet the fact remains that two times already the Lottery Commission has called to tell him he has won. Really it is too much! Philip comes downstairs fresh and clean to assure Lynn it was not the Lottery Commission calling, but hardly has he begun to speak when Lynn puts on a startled look, then fans the breath of his words away, squinting. This is to remind Philip that she is mad at him for coming home stewed, then snoring with his mouth open and contracting horse breath. "Can't we just have a nice, suburban breakfast conversation?" he asks. Adam stops spinning a toy globe on the kitchen table to look at his father reasonably. "Yes, Dad," he says.

———◇———

It is that time in late spring when the flowers from all the flowering trees are coming down, seemingly at once. The pink flowers from the crab apples. The ivory-white flowers from the catalpas, and the foaming creamy ones from the chestnuts. Philip rubs a spot clear in the kitchen window to look out at all the petals roiled up in his front yard like surf. A poisoned arrow of desire makes him suddenly wish to sculpt it. More poisoned arrows make him wish to sculpt other things, as well: his love for his wife, Lynn; his love for their son, dressed in his Spiderman shirt; maybe even something about the phone call that wasn't; but he knows he cannot. He is simply too—

———◇———

Outside, where Philip takes Adam on a sudden passion in the middle of breakfast, all the flowering trees are enjoying the last fullness of their bloom but one. The dogwood is a late bloomer, every year. Philip lifts Adam by the waist and holds him around his Spiderman shirt to look at a bud. "That's a bud," he teaches. "What do you suppose will be inside it when it opens?" Adam stares at the bud for some time. Then he turns to his father and says, "Birds?"

———◇———

Stagestruck. Stage fright. Philip keeps getting these two terms mixed up. In painful letters to gallery owners across the nation, in desperate late-night phone calls to critics, Philip keeps forgetting which means terror of displaying

145

your stuff before the public, which means aching to. Stagestruck. Stage fright. How can he speak of his plight, this overloaded lottery winner, when the terms keep clotting together like that?

———◇———

Schedule for the morning: Philip will drive Lynn to her law school, he will drive Adam to the day-care wing of the law school, he will try to grab some sleep in one of the empty day-care rooms, he will see his psychiatrist, he will pick up Adam at day care, he will come home to wreck some more designs. Philip goes to warm up the car, waving away an imaginary fly.

———◇———

"Do you have a hangover?"
"You know I do."
"Were you at Margy's?"
"You know I was."
"Is it an absolutely anguishing hangover?"

———◇———

Lynn has not always been a law student. Once she was a ballet dancer. She was a beautiful ballet dancer but she was shy. She would not let Philip see her dance, even after they were married. Philip would play the piano while she danced behind him, unseen. Philip used to love hearing her joints crack behind him, seeing her white reflection whirling in the dark mahogany of the piano wood. But that was as close as he got. Shortly after the second big lottery win Lynn put away her dancing slippers, bought a briefcase for law school. Philip was chagrined. "Why let the money make you serious?" he asked. "Aren't you serious about your sculptures?" she countered. "I've always been serious about my sculptures," he shouted, "and being serious isn't helping one bit!" Philip had a sudden urge, then, to cough into his napkin. "Would you mind passing the yogurt, please?" he had said.

———◇———

Margy is a ballet dancer. She used to be a registered nurse, but now she is a ballet dancer. She used to be the nurse who helped deliver Adam—Philip still remembers her little round white nails on Lynn's tanned belly as she and Philip put their faces together to watch the baby head crown—but then she accepted Philip's grateful present of orchids for the smooth delivery. She accepted his invitation to have capuccino in the hospital cafeteria. And now she is a ballet dancer, living on Philip's lottery money. She has no problem letting Philip support her with his lottery money. She has no problem letting Philip watch her dance. In fact, she would like to dance for him nude—*anything*—but Philip won't allow himself the pleasure. All he will allow is to sit and give her back rubs and feel sorry for what a rotten series of boyfriends she has had.

———◇———

"More brown sugar or less brown sugar?" "Coming in or going out?" These are the questions put to Philip during breakfast, and Philip fields them like a pro. "Less," he says—just like that. "Out," he says, clicking the door shut against the springtime mosquitoes. Why can't he be this decisive in the rest of his life? A crater of pink plastic here, a sprout of steel girders there. A decision not to skip this morning's psychiatric appointment, a decision not to break down and buy another lottery ticket; but he knows, as he approaches his guilty reflection in the window of the car, he knows that he just—

———◇———

Adam has the toy globe with him in his car seat. He is spinning it and spinning it as Philip puts the car in reverse.

Then, when Philip puts the car in forward, Adam stops spinning the globe. He puts his index finger on the blue expanse of the Atlantic. "This is the Atlantic," he says reasonably. He puts his index finger on Austin, Texas. "This is New York," he says, also reasonably.

———◇———

Philip and Lynn and Adam have to pass under a suburban city hall to get to the law building. They used to be nervous about driving under it, because a reporter friend of theirs said all the construction workers were on angel dust when they built it. But this morning as they pass beneath the city hall Philip realizes they have been nervous for the wrong reason. Not because of imminent collapse, but simply because it is one more spot on the earth where families pass with their troubles.

———◇———

"I'm sorry for fanning your breath away," Lynn says, as the law building looms. "It was a rude thing to do. Besides, you don't even have horse breath. You have wonderful breath, if you want to know." They pull up in front of her law school, but Lynn does not get out. She is starting to cry, to put her arms around Philip and to make Philip cry, too. "That's the problem," she says, "I love your breath. That's the problem," she says, "you're breaking my heart."

———◇———

This is what Philip would like to say to Adam, on the half-block ride to the day-care wing. "Adam, Mommy and I were not actually crying. Actually, we were practicing for a commedia dell'arte we're going to be in one of these days. Actually, we were fairly happy while we were pretending to be crying. There is nothing wrong and there never will be. Mommy will be safe, and Daddy will be safe, and we will all live happily ever after, forever."

———◇———

This is an opposite thing that Philip would like to say to Adam: "Adam, Mommy is sad because she's a basically monogamous person and I'm a basically monogamous person but sometimes I need to let off a little steam. That's why I have a mistress. But I only sleep with her a teeny bit! I give her back rubs, in fact—but strictly through her shirt. Luckily, in our day and age, it is perfectly reasonable for a man who loves his wife to stay out half the night giving back rubs to another woman through her shirt."

———◇———

One time Adam burst into his parents' bedroom at two o'clock in the morning, shouting, "What's for breakfast?" When Philip had to tell Adam that breakfast would not take place for several hours more, Adam looked crushed. Adam has really dark eyes. He has really large tears when he cries. His tears don't fall from his eyes; they spring. That is why on the half-block ride from law school to the day-care wing, Philip chooses to say nothing at all.

———◇———

The day-care teacher takes Philip into a glass-walled room to talk over his child with him. They sit in day-care chairs, pink and blue. The day-care teacher is very petite and she wears a frilly little dress that exposes the upper parts of her arms, which are spongy. She has nice eyes, though, that blink a lot when she talks. She tells Philip that Adam is a darling boy. She says can Philip keep a secret? That Adam is her favorite pupil this year. She tells Philip that Adam is exceptionally well-coordinated and that he is strong. His tug-of-war is coming along nicely, she says, he is B plus at rolling, B plus at climbing, A plus at jumping from high places . . . Philip watches the petite day-care teacher blink with admiration as she reels off

Adam's attributes from her day-care chair. He is blinking, too.

———◇———

Of course it is also true that when he was twenty, Philip had a one-man show of his designs in New York. Yes, he used to feel natural. His stage fright did not click in till later. But at that time, at the time of his one-man show, his garret roommate, an unemployed pastry chef, was blasé. The garret-mate saw nothing unusual about the fact that Philip's environmental designs were scheduled to fill wall after wall, four of the glitziest art showrooms of New York. He watched Philip going over the proofs of the brochure, and said nothing. Page after page of black-and-white photos of Philip's designs, on glossy paper. Then he saw Philip take out a magic marker and carefully draw an arrow from one page to the other, signifying that he chose to reverse two photos. The unemployed pastry chef was aghast. "You mean to tell me," he said, shaking his head and blinking with admiration of an unhealthy sort, "you get to redo the order of the brochure?"

———◇———

To grab some sleep, Philip lies on the carpet of an unused day-care room. When he closes his eyes, huge hangover pictures fill his brain—pictures of huge white ants walking toward his face through the strands of green carpet. The strands of green carpet are like a jungle but they are being trampled by the huge white ants. The strands of green carpet may be junglelike but they are no match for the huge white ants. It is a pushover. There is not even a contest. Philip wakes with a start. "What contest?" he says.

———◇———

Philip decides his hangover is too bad to go see his psychiatrist. He walks outside in the day-care corridor to use the pay phone. He calls the number. The busy signal nearly snaps his eardrum. He calls again, holding the receiver half a length away, until he is sure he hears ringing. He puts the receiver to his ear, and again the busy signal nearly snaps his eardrum. Philip decides this is a sign that he had better go see his psychiatrist.

———◇———

The route from the day care—law school to the psychiatrist's house passes Margy's house. Sometimes when he passes this way he sees Margy walking out her front door with a mountain of dirty laundry in her arms. It alarms Philip to think how frequently he sees her this way, in fact. It offends his sense of romance. He would like to have a romantic picture of his mistress, even if he does refuse to sleep with her. He would like to think that buds opened up to reveal—

———◇———

What a rotten series of boyfriends Margy has had, thinks Philip, in the waiting room at the back of the psychiatrist's immense sober house. One of them named Tony used to punch himself in the face whenever they had a fight. Tony busted his own nose when she broke up with him. Another one named Ahmed after a gallant courtship scooped her up to carry her into the bedroom, but he slipped on the linoleum and busted Margy's elbow. And now Margy has Philip. Philip doesn't bust anything. Philip doesn't bust one goddamn thing.

———◇———

The psychiatrist comes a little closer, this time, to convincing Philip that he is not a chicken person. He only uses cowardice as a cover. It's not cowardice that keeps him from sleeping with Margy, it's anger—he wants to punish himself. It's not cowardice that keeps him from doing environmental sculptures—but then what is it? Why can't Philip jump from high places? This is the question

Philip silently asks himself. He silently asks himself this question while lying on the psychiatrist's suburban couch when he's supposed to be talking, gesticulating. He silently asks himself this question while listening to the sound of the psychiatrist's suburban dishwasher on its rinse cycle in another part of the immense sober house. The sound of the psychiatrist's suburban dishwasher on its rinse cycle makes Philip feel unbelievably superfluous to the world, unbelievably irrelevant. Jump? he says to himself. I hardly dare to breathe.

—————◇—————

Is gallantry still alive in the 1980's? Philip wonders this, also, while listening to the dishwasher on its rinse cycle in another part of the psychiatrist's house. When Margy's old boyfriend Ahmed tried to be gallant, he slipped on the linoleum. Did boyfriends slip on linoleum in, say, the 1940's? More to the point—did phones ring you out of your sleep with no one on the other end in the 1940's? For Philip's phone had acted strangely last time, too—the last time he was out drinking rum zombies half the night with Margy. Someone was there, that time—the local federal penitentiary calling. "Are you guards coming to work today or not?" asked someone who identified himself as the warden. Philip was forced to explain through his hangover that he was not a prison guard. "You're not?" barked the warden furiously. "Well then," he barked, before hanging up, "I suppose you think I have the wrong number?"

—————◇—————

"You mean to tell me you stayed out till four-fifteen giving her a *back rub*?" the psychiatrist asks gently. Too gently. Philip thinks about this. He wonders if it's worth it to add that he also gave her a foot massage—though strictly through her leotards. He wonders if he should mention lying on opposite sides of her sofa, fondling the nubbly cuffs of her blue warm-ups, the loose golden thread . . . Horrifyingly, however, Philip hears himself give off a snore. He shakes himself, but not in time. He is petrified, aflame. Falling asleep on a psychiatrist's couch, he comprehends immediately, is something that may mortally and forever offend his sense of romance.

———◇———

Philip sits up with a start. Passion overtakes him. "My God!" he cries. "Here I am, with two women! I need more than two women! I need six women! I need two dozen women! And still it won't be enough to save me from being locked in here! In this horrible place! I'm in a huge, echoing, money-filled space, with nothing for company but my designs for a diseased planet, and I'm screaming, and no one can hear me!"

"I'm afraid it *is* time for us to conclude today," the psychiatrist says gently.

———◇———

There is always Adam. Philip remembers Adam this morning in the car running his forefinger slowly around the globe's equator. Philip could tell that Adam was having serious thoughts about seeing his parents cry. It must have been frightening to see them cry, but Adam did not reveal his fright. He put his forefinger in his mouth, slowly, to see if he could taste the equator that way. He couldn't. With a sudden passion, Philip rushes to pick up Adam from day-care. A concrete wall surrounds the sunken day-care playground. Philip rushes up to the wall, exhausted. He may not work this afternoon. He deserves a rest. Pick up a batch of lottery tickets, maybe—why the hell not? Why not hundreds of them, to make a bed for himself and his two women, and forget the rest? Philip puts his head over the wall and like a magnet his eye is drawn down to a little boy in a Spiderman shirt. Of all the dozens of kids in the playground, his eye is drawn irretrievably to this one. Adam stands alone atop a high wooden picnic table. He is swinging his arms. From way up over the wall Philip sees Adam's mouth counting, and as Adam begins his jump through space, Philip's lungs are filled with wind, and he gasps.

BETRAYING JILLY

At ten of four in the morning Owen awoke from a condition of dreaming deep inside his sleep and walked to the
beach door of the rented cottage bedroom and stood out
on the small wooden deck over the sand. Owen stood on
the deck for thirty seconds, for forty seconds, feeling the
wind, and then he woke up more, and he saw the Northern Lights: a silver shimmering in the sky far out over the
lake. Part of it was a silver shimmering and part of it was a
silver fog, with lights like police lights shining straight up
into the night as if some perfect crime had been com-
mitted—some spectacular bank heist, Owen thought, or
some gloriously just Robin Hood holdup—and then he
woke up further, and he remembered that he had very
likely gotten his wife pregnant five hours earlier. He

turned on the ball of one foot and called back through the screen door, "Want to see the Northern Lights?" but he called it softly, because he sensed this was one of the things Jilly would not want to be awakened for, and he waited an instant before returning to the sky and the lake and the Lights. It was his first Northern Lights and it thrilled him, made him feel daring to his bones.

Owen came inside from the deck and he stood over the bed admiring his wife's sleep. She had a perfect sleep. It was not the sleep of newspaper swirling in the streets but of cotton growing in the fields, of cotton lace growing up in rows, if that were possible. She had a beautiful sleep. Owen looked down at her and he grew more sharply awake, and he lifted the sheet and looked at the fair length of her, and wondered if he should sink into the bed and begin to seize gently with his hands. Then he decided wait, wait—a treat made better by delay—and he put the sheet back. With a quickening of excitement he noticed for the first time that they had been sleeping their entire month here in the shadows, out of the gracious orange glow of the electric clock, and he turned the clock so that it faced in toward the bed, like a soft spotlight on a wedding scene. He sat in the wicker rocking chair with his feet on a suitcase and he listened to the night sounds: the creaking of the cottage roof that he liked; the far-off foghorn from Skilagalee, a soggy sound that had not quit the entire month and had gone deep inside his ears. Sometimes he could hear Skilagalee when it wasn't sounding. That was how deep inside his ears the foghorn had gone.

Then the night sounds faded and a day sound sprang up—a chipmunk stepping on a dead twig—and Owen felt his ear cock toward it as human ears must have cocked a hundred thousand years ago. A fly bumped into the screen of the east window, first part of the room to be warmed by the coming sun. Minoltas hung everywhere in the new light. Across the room the glass table became visible with all the Scrabble letters downturned like a genetic code.

———◇———

This was their last day; Owen decided to get up. He drew on his white seersucker bathing suit over his darkened skin and opened the door onto the dim hallway, and across the hallway he quietly turned the knob to his son's room and looked inside at Jake, who had his hands over his head like a ballet dancer and was wearing a very complex expression in the pebbly glow of the night-light. The mobile of boats above his head fluttered with the sudden cross-draft. Owen closed the door, went downstairs, made coffee, picked up a copy of the ferry schedule and sat in front of the picture window to read it. The coffee tasted peculiar; Owen opened the door and pitched most of it onto the sand. He went around the living room with the ferry schedule, breaking up cobwebs that had formed during the night. The month long he had seen nothing but daddy longlegs, which Owen considered surely too aristocratic for such work. Where were the crumpled little spiders, the movers and shakers that got things done? Owen himself felt pleased that he had done so much all month— photos presenting themselves right and left! He'd been on a roll, and all of it was lubricated by the activity of doing nothing—nothing but swim and chase cottontails over the dunes and think about his dad.

A ladybug landed on the fly of his bathing suit when he stepped outside and stood on the patio. Without thinking, Owen flicked it to the sand, where it landed on its back, scurried aright, and took off with a flabbergasted air. A tiny magnificent green-and-red bug landed almost at once on the same part of his suit, and Owen let it be. He watched the air fill slowly with spectral light: dawn clouds pink as salmon scales around last night's moon sheared in half as if by a paper cutter. He fiddled with his wedding band so that he could look at the untanned mark. Then suddenly feeling famished, he jumped off the patio and walked down the dunes that were ice-cold to his feet.

And as he swam in the cold white water he thought about his dad some more. He thought about the time they had taken a walk down Crockett Street together—he a boy and his father a young man—and he had asked his dad whether, if he really needed to, he could make his marriage last forever—forever and ever, and never have to leave for another woman. The question had made his dad impatient. "What do you mean, if I really needed to?" he demanded. Then the question began to excite him. "Oh well, if you mean, really needed, if I had to, I suppose so, I suppose I could, *yes*." So his father had thought of his marriage as perfect.

Owen had always thought of his own marriage as nearly perfect. He had thought, sometimes, that when he settled down and became a father, then it might be perfectly perfect, whatever that was. But here he was a father, a father perhaps twice over, and still he wondered sometimes if something might be missing. The truth, of course, the cry-ing-out-loud truth, was that in the end his father had left his mother for a home-office secretary of Barnum and Bailey. He had given Owen his first camera before leaving.

Owen swam all the way out to the sandbar on a crawl, then turned on his side for the return trip. When he got halfway to the shore he felt cramped, a panic in his stom-ach, and he flipped to his back to float. For the duration of eight long waves he lay on his back, letting the panic pass, the cramp of fear retreat . . . finally he hit the shore, gasp-ing. He hauled himself out of the water and collapsed on the sand with his knees bent, making an easy target for the sun which was newly risen, pale as a bubble against the pink sky. Then he decided to get up. Then he decided wait, wait; and he unzipped his bathing suit and lay down with his feet toward the water and closed his eyes and wondered if something really was missing. "Yes," he said aloud—but only to see how it sounded. Everything would be all right, he told himself; none of the things that could go wrong in the world would go wrong. Thirstily he gripped the sand. The sun came higher and the light flew all about, but gradually it spread out and the world turned yellow around the edges as Owen seemed to fall asleep. He dreamed.

He dreamed a beautiful woman was standing over him, dressed head to toe in a bright gold kangaroo suit. "*Pardonnez*," she said. "But do you happen to know where there's a women's room?"

"Oh!" Owen said. His hand flew down to check his suit, then up to shield his eyes. Absurdly, he felt the back of his head rise several inches off the sand. "What kind of women's room?" he asked, squinting.

"What kind of women's room," the woman repeated slowly. She pondered, removing first one gold glove, then the other, causing a delicate amount of sand to sprinkle down on top of Owen. She smiled lewdly. "We've been to an all-night party," she replied.

Behind her, Owen could make out another beautiful woman in a gold canary suit, waiting like an orgasm to explode.

"Is your friend looking for one, too?" Owen heard himself ask.

Still fixing him with her bold, dirty smile, the woman in the kangaroo suit answered this ridiculous question by dropping both gloves to the sand beside Owen's shoulder. Her head rocked with the force of a sudden hiccup. "She's looking for anything she can get," she whispered conspiratorially.

Realizing with impossible clarity that they were drunk, and had been drunk for months, waiting for him to be lying here like this, Owen brushed a particle of sand off the tip of his nose, off the point of his chin, composing himself. "Yes, well," he said, "there are restrooms at the beach club, of course. If you go back the way you came, hang left for about—"

Somewhere in the middle of his over-conscientious directions the kangaroo-woman slithered to the sand in a loamy heap that covered Owen and she began to sting his mouth with deep, sucky kisses. The canary-woman in the background jumped once and clapped her hands with glee—but not before Owen had managed to sit upright and, like a dream going too slow, shove the kangaroo-woman away.

The kangaroo-woman looked at him with an expression that was raunchy, patient, perfectly sure of itself, and the slightest bit amused.

"Don't tell me," the kangaroo-woman said. "You've already *got* a kangaroo. Right? That you love and cherish? And keep locked up in a cage at home?" She hiccuped again, then undid the kangaroo shoulder strap to scratch at her suddenly naked breast. *"Pardonnez,"* she said. "This fuzz has been driving me crazy all night."

Owen looked at her breast, burnished gold so it glowed.

"Do you realize I'm an oracle?" the kangaroo-woman persisted, kissing her index finger before dabbing it to his chin.

Owen blushed golden.

"You know: Like in those Greek plays," she elaborated, "who can tell you about your present life, and predict things that are going to befall you?"

The canary-woman in the background batted her hands together, then began plumping up her tail feathers behind her in a silent courtship dance.

"Sure," said the kangaroo-woman. "Thus I predict you're going to lose your kangaroo and any kangarooettes you may have."

Supernatural sweepings of sand were flying from her hair. Her face blew in and out of the sun. The kangaroo-woman picked up one glove teasingly and tilted her chin to regard Owen. "You know, I don't really have to find the women's room," she said. "An oracle has no needs! An oracle is not flesh and blood! We only like to provide this free service, of telling people what's surely going to hap—"

Owen arched forward with his cock. Fully expecting it, the kangaroo-woman gave a little gasp and gulped forward to take it in her mouth—erect gold in her soft golden mouth. The canary woman dropped behind to suck him in turn, the two of them tugging goldly as Owen went dizzy for eight seconds, for twelve seconds—when just as dizzily he stopped and pulled back. "I'm not going to lose my family," he panted.

There seemed to be only one woman now, whirling to a freeze. She kissed his tip once, then turned back slowly, with eyes that were *very* amused. "Honey, you just did," she winked, and hardly were the words dry in the air when with a shiver the bright light failed. Owen awakened himself with a shock.

Owen waited a moment while a scarflike cloud was drawn across the boiling white coin of the sun and then, when the sun had come back, he rezipped his bathing suit and plunged inside the water, going under for three strokes and making a gurgling breathless sound that was a little like the sound of drowning—but not really like the sound of drowning. When he came up out of the thousand dazzling dimes of water there was a bee, a hornet, floating on the surface that Owen felt urgent about saving. He cupped it in a handful of water and began charging noisily for shore, but he let the water splash free upon noticing— with sudden renewed quiet—the hornet had already died. Unhurriedly, he began breast-stroking toward the beach when he saw two new figures flipping slowly down the dunes—but who were *these* apparitions; what dream might *they* propose? Neither was dressed in golden kangaroo clothes, so far as he could tell. One of them was a great deal larger than the other. And then—oh, he knew. They were Jilly and the boy, Jake, and they were waving, the whites of their hands flashing like the bottom-sides of fish, and Owen was waving back, coming in, climbing out, standing by them and scaring Jake a little bit by how much water was dripping off him. Some of the drops fell on Jake as Owen kissed Jilly.

"Morning," Jilly said. Her manner was filled with a devotion that seemed deadly; sleep marks like the long scar of a cotton flower wrinkled her pale cheek.

Owen faced her, opaque with weariness; he wanted to protest, but instead took a faded towel from his wife's hands and breathed evenly, rubbing the wet ends of hair around his ears. "Morning," he said. "Thank you."

"For what?"

"Towel."

Jilly plucked at his elbow with a squeeze that was meant to feel secret. "Anytime," she said. She smiled fervently.

Involuntarily, Owen took a step back. He cleared one half of his throat. "You ask Jake? If he's ready for a little sister?"

They looked at him.

"I did," Jilly said. "And he says he wants a little brother."

"You bet," said Jake.

162

"Oh? A little brother would be more your style?" Owen asked, bending down and taking hold of Jake's waist. But Jake squealed, then, and pulled loose to clasp his mother's knee.

"Jake's a little sleepy this morning," Jilly told Owen.

"Are you, Jake? Is that what it is?"

"No."

"What's wrong, then?"

Jake shrugged, taking hold of his penis.

"Ah," Owen said. He switched the towel to his neck and chest. "You want to make lightning on the sand, but you want your dad to help you. Right?"

"You bet," Jake said. "Thunder, too."

"No. You made thunder just last night," Owen said.

Jilly smiled. "You guys," she said, claiming them with affection.

Owen led Jake to a sandy mound where a juniper bush was dying. He tugged down Jake's shorts and aimed him. In a second there was the sound like the sound of plants being watered, but with a carbonated-fizz quality to it. Jake finished making his lightning. "I like you, Daddy," he said.

"I like *you*, Jake," said Owen. He smiled fully, then, his first real smile of the morning, and hitched up Jake's shorts to lead him back when all at once he saw Jilly pick up an old discarded glove from the sand, and regard it curiously like the finger of crime. "Oh!" he said then, pouncing to flip the thing out of sight, then gripping their shoulders with sudden ferocity. "I want this family to be perfect. I want us always to adore each other and stay happy and never to break each other's hearts. I've got such a hopeless crush on you two!" he cried. "I love you both so much!"

There was a pause.

"Why 'hopeless?'" asked Jilly.
There was another pause. Something rustled.
"Look!" Jake told his father. "A cottontail!"
The two of them broke loose to give chase.
Jilly turned on one foot in time to see them vanish behind a dune. "Why 'hopeless?'" she called, softly.

STRANGER
IN THE HOUSE

It had been a late fall, raining warm rain for two weeks, so that when the air finally cleared, cool as crystal, the leaves on all the trees began turning color at once, tentatively at first, then with increasing glory—the fiery sycamore trees, the deep-orange maples—and then the warm rain had returned, washing them down in a heap. It was discouraging to look out and see the little yard foamy with foliage, the windows actually smeared with bright wet plant life. Inside the raw kitchen, Andrew had his third cold of the season. Vicki, however, wasn't having colds this year. She was too *excited* to have colds: with her life, say, or the weather, or the holiday (it was Halloween), or the fact that she was leaving momentarily for Boston to see a matinee. Andrew gaped at the charged new presence of this woman who for years had been too much the opposite of charged: calling him at his office to absorb some of his energy, clinging to his passion which, once unleashed, was big enough for two. But now suddenly in her sleep she was wiggling her toes. Even having a quick late-morning lunch she commanded such manic attention that Andrew found himself breathless for his half of the conversation. And when she was gone to her Boston matinees these days, her absence left holes too big for him and his son to fill. She was leaving holes now, talking about their son's first trick-or-treat costume.

"No, we'd better *not* dress him as one of those old men in greasy green raincoats," she was saying, "because that's probably what he'll turn *into* in real life. The kind in restaurants who're always waiting to use the phone? When you have to walk by on the way to the bathroom? Creepy Masher. Of course, on the other hand, there's a chance he'll be . . . Toscanini! You think? What sort of old man do you suppose he'll be?"

Andrew took of his glasses to blow his nose for the thirtieth time. He put his glasses right in the circle of apple sauce. "Creepy Masher," he said.

"Or forget 'old man,'" Vicki was saying. "It's bad enough just to imagine what kind of twenty-one-year-old he'll be. Surly Rocker, I bet. They're all Surly Rockers at twenty-one, aren't they?"

"We sure as hell were."

"Oh, please, please, Lord, don't make him Surly Rocker," Vicki said. Matter-of-factly, but with a faraway considering expression, she picked up Andrew's glasses and awed him by licking the sauce from the lenses. "Or okay, make him Surly Rocker," she decided, "but please, I beg of you, Lord, don't make him Sullen Punk. I could not take Sullen Punk."

"You thinking about when he's sixteen?"

"Sixteen and hating his parents. We'll ask him what he

needs the car for and he'll roll his eyes." Vicki's head shuddered with the force of a sudden hiccup—the apple sauce itself commanding attention deep inside her throat—and she put Andrew's glasses down. I could not *take* rolling eyes," she said. "If we're only raising him so he can roll his eyes at us, I say forget it. I say never mind, take it all back."

"'Take it all back?'"

Vicki looked at him with eyes that narrowed sharply at his suspiciousness. "No. Of course not 'take it all back,'" she said.

Her eyes widened as two-year-old Matt entered the room with a small silk pillowcase over his head.

"Anyway," Andrew said, "he sure makes a great Baby Ghost, doesn't he?"

Vicki didn't say anything. Her eyes were round as she watched Matt walk gently into the wall, turn, and walk gently into the door.

Andrew picked up a napkin to wipe his watery, sore eyes. His mind, soggy with flu, was plodding. "No, of course not all kids turn sour," he said. "Some kids don't drift away, right? Relationships with children have got at least as much chance as relationships with adults, don't you think? What?"

"Where's Matt?" Vicki was whispering. She was holding Matt in her arms and whispering through the pillowcase, as Matt squealed with pleasure. "Is he *here*?" she whispered, poking. "Is he *here*?"

Andrew turned his napkin inside out to blow his nose for the thirty-first time. "That's the trouble with not being able to smell anything," he said. "Everything smells like vanishing cream."

———◇———

When the dishes were done, Andrew stood Matt on the windowsill of the kitchen overlooking the driveway, and both of them looked solemnly at the old Plymouth warming up. They were transfixed—Matt with his thumb in his mouth, his silk pillowcase pressed softly to one eye—by the clouds of carbon monoxide that chugged out from the vibrating tail pipe into the cold wetness of the autumn afternoon, obscuring at intervals the sight of red and black leaves plastered across the car's windows . . . obscuring and then revealing. Vicki rushed into the kitchen from the stairs in her lined raincoat, and she put her arms around Andrew and Matt. They both stared at her rather plain, forthright face, arranged as if on purpose to look poignant in the dark, and smelling, piercingly, of eagerness.

"So long," she said, kissing them equally. "You take care of yourselves."

"Take care of *yourself*," said Andrew. "Slow down. It's slippery out there."

"Sure," said Vicki—then shot him a worried look.

"Mommy?" said Matt.

"What, honey?"

Matt put out his arms and began to cry. "Don't."

"Mom's just going into Boston for the matinee," explained Andrew, as Vicki watched with a wavering smile. "First she goes away, and then she comes back when we're both howling maniacs," he explained. "Do you want to watch her leave in the car?"

"Ya," Matt said.

"Okay," said Andrew. Vicki came forward again and touched her fragrant lips to Andrew's, then to Matt's. "First we give her a kiss," Andrew said—Vicki withdrew and glided out the door—"and now we get to witness the wiles of womankind."

They both stared as Vicki clicked lightly across the cobblestones, climbed in, and arranged her coat around her ankles. The door shut them away from her, but through the dark and leafy car window they could see a shoulder harness being worked about, a small white hand blowing kisses from a face that looked, frighteningly, as if it had lived a hundred years ago, and had long ago been removed from the face of the earth. "Don't!" thought Andrew—but the car backed away.

At the kitchen window, Andrew was moved to be left with the reflection of his ring hand on Matt's dark hair.

"Now," said Andrew, taking Matt by the fingers and letting him swing to his hip, then catching him around the waist, "let's curb our existential whatchamacallit, and see what we can find to do."

Next to a bloated pumpkin in the living room, Matt sat in Andrew's lap and they looked at pictures of dinosaur bones in the Sunday *Globe*.

"What's that guy doin'?" Matt asked.

"He's holding up a label. See, they're all holding up labels and sticking them to the bones."

"A, B, C, D," recited Matt.

"Good," said Andrew. He was silently reading through the first paragraph of the article; and in a minute Matt had slipped off his lap and was trodding around the living room, saying "A, B, Q, R, N, B." But a minute later he had his arm under the lid of the pumpkin and was brutalizing the carved teeth.

"Matt!" yelled Andrew.

"No!" yelled Matt. "Don't touch!"

"You know—you know I don't want you to touch that," Andrew said. His throat was beginning to ache again, and he cleared it gingerly for a long time. "Why don't you go play something on the piano?" he suggested.

A minute later the pumpkin teeth were brutalized again. "*Matt!*"

Matt yanked back his hand in fear and surprise. His

body stiffened—all thirty-two inches of it—he pointed the criminal hand at his father and yelled at the top of his voice: "NO!"

Andrew gazed at him, less stern than wondrous. "Do you want me to play with you?" he asked at last.

"Ya," said Matt cheerfully, propping himself onto the back of the couch with his elbows and swinging his feet in their strawberry socks.

Matt sat on his father's lap at the piano, bopping the middle-range notes with a blue plastic cube; Andrew played a rag around the cube so that the rag wasn't all there and much was there that shouldn't have been, but still it was a bright and hopeful sound for a darkening fall afternoon. Presently, however, Matt began to sweep his father's hands off the keys.

"Can't I play, too?" Andrew asked, peering around at the boy's face. With the blue plastic cube, Matt slugged him hard enough to dislodge his glasses.

Andrew sprang to his feet, hauling the child halfway across the room. "Do you want to be punished?" he bellowed. "What is the matter with you?"

"Bad Matt," Matt said.

Andrew straightened his glasses, squinting at the way it rocked the room back to normal. Then he took a deep breath and said, "No. Matt's not bad. Matt's just unsettled without knowing where his mother is, maybe, and it's time to go down for a nap. Do you want to take a nap?"

"Ya."

"What do you know," Andrew said, exhaling. "Now look," he said, turning off the light, then feeling his way about the dark living room with Matt in his arms, and through the empty guest room, and along the cold front hallway, looking for Matt's special pillowcase. "I'm going to take a nap, too. Just because your mother took off again doesn't mean we're going to miss her so much we can't sleep, right?" They found the pillowcase under the kitchen table, next to the sleeping dog, and Andrew snapped it in the air a couple of times to get the hairs off.

"Good Daddy," Matt said, taking the worn silk in one hand, putting his thumb in his mouth, and locking his cool head against his father's breast. Andrew got them both up the hollow staircase with a smile, and placed Matt down in his crib. "Let's be pals forever," he whispered, kissing the soft spot just back of his eye, and closing the door.

Andrew stripped off all his clothes and swung into bed. The pillow was chilled from the picture window just over the bed, but Andrew squeezed it under his head and re-laxed. With his glasses off, his eyes closed, he could feel his cold trying to organize itself into a fever, trying to erect a cottony screen between his head and the outside world, but Andrew accepted the sensation, knowing he was going to break the screen, sleep it down. He began to dream that a hundred phantoms, a hundred families, were lying naked on a beach, very close together, on hot sand near the sound of water.

The door banged open.

Matt was standing in the doorway, draping his pil-lowcase on the floor behind him.

Andrew sat up in bed, astonished. "How did you get out of your crib?" he asked.

"He climbed out," Matt said.

"I see that he climbed out, but he'd better get back in it right now," Andrew said. Sorely, nakedly, Andrew rose, scooped Matt up and replaced him in his crib, closing the two doors between them—and resettled into bed, finding the same beach, the same phantoms, except that the cen-tral character, himself, was trembling this time. A man with a stranger's face was lying between him and his wife

171

on the sand. "Why are you trembling?" the man asked. "Because today I feel extinct!" he answered—but just then a wave came crashing before them on the sand. Andrew lurched awake.

"Matt!" he said, heaving out of bed for the second time and roughly carrying the boy back to his crib. "I don't want you to climb out anymore. Take a nap, forget your anxieties, and *then* I'll get you out. Understand?"

The beach was gone.

Andrew lay on his side, facing Matt's room. His bed-sheets were wrinkled, his eyelids twitched—and behind his eyelids loomed a huge vision of railroad track, fore-shortened as though he were something tiny, about to be run over by a rampaging freight. Almost immediately he heard the squeak of a small mattress, and he went in to find Matt lowering himself from the bars, the tips of his strawberry socks only inches from the floor.

"This is not a joke," Andrew said, pulling him from the bars, yanking his socks off, and standing Matt before him. "Do you want to get hit?"

"No," Matt said.

"Are you going to stay in bed?"

"No," Matt said.

Andrew took his son's left hand and tapped it, setting off shock waves throughout the room. Matt peered at his father to puzzle out why he would want to hurt his hand. He tried to laugh, but something had for the first time turned foul.

Andrew deposited him in his crib. "Lie there," he said. "Lie there, and don't move, or I'll hit you again."

"Bad Daddy!" shouted Matt, in anger.

Andrew sank to his knees before the crib, pressing his blurry eyes to the bars. Then he rose. Steadily he took the boy's left arm and delivered it three even smacks, astonishing Matt so greatly that Andrew had time to lay him down, walk back to his room—stepping on one of Matt's squealing toys on the way—and get back into bed in breathless silence before the wails came.

Matt wailed and sobbed for a long time. Andrew lay in bed remembering what his boy looked like in tears, his black eyes glistening—olives slippery with oil. He remembered the early days, the first time he ever saw his son yawn; incredibly, it had made Andrew yawn, too—proof that the boy was real. And the 3 A.M. nursings, mother and son suffused in the glow of the night light, so there was only a minute difference between the lavender of her flannel and the turquoise of his. As the sobs from the next room softened, and he turned more deeply into the cool splendor of his bed, Andrew wondered how long he would remember these things. He wondered how long he would remember the other things, too, the small betrayals: how long he would remember Matt last Halloween entrusting him with his candied-apple treat, and Andrew, wanting to protect Matt's teeth, quickly flushing it down the disposal; how long he would remember he himself entrusting into Matt's delicate cupped hands his Halloween carnation, and coming back five minutes later to find the carnation busted, shredded, lying in a pool of its own black-and-orange petals—and Andrew thought then about the terrible burden of innocence people brought to their dealings with each other, parents and children every bit as much as parents and parents. All that trust. All that tenderness. For a long while he thought about that, and then he sighed, and luxuriated in the gradual accumulation of silence, until, very tenuously, the whimpering began again, and came closer.

"Daddy," Matt said, rubbing his left arm gravely as he stood in the open doorway, "he wants you to get up."

In the soft gray light of their womanless afternoon together, Andrew put out his arms for the boy to come closer. He hoisted Matt onto his bed, and gave his nose a very long, a very nice, squeeze. "Matt," he said, "it's too early to get up. Don't you see? If you let your worries get the best of you now, you'll have no faith in people, you'll grow up hating the world, and next thing you know you'll be one of those guys standing around in a greasy green raincoat."

"Get up, please."

"Baby," Andrew said. "I appreciate your loneliness. Seriously I do. But even if these matinees last two months, and she falls in love with her leading man, she's bound to get over it: She'll never leave us alone for good. So," he said, rising, carrying the tired boy and his pillowcase—and lowered him down to his crib amid a crowd of stuffed animals. Then at last, his head between two argyle alligators, the boy seemed to accept. He took his thumb in his mouth, blinked his eyes a couple of times in slow motion. His eyelids got heavier as his father smiled down at him, smoothing his long wavy hair away from his brow. "Sleep well, old man," he said.

Back in his room, Andrew adjusted the gauzy curtains on the picture window, straightened out the much-abused bedding, and curled into a tight, surrendering ball—when he heard the squeak.

Ripping the pillowcase from Matt's grasp and slamming it into his face, Andrew was distinctly aware of muffled screaming, distinctly aware of helpless thrashing. Then, flinging the pillowcase across the room, Andrew released Matt and hurled him white-faced to the mattress. He towered over him in his naked rage while the boy screeched in terror, while he took his thumb gaspingly . . . then dropped with a shudder to sleep; just like that, the tears drying on his cheeks, the childhood colors returning, an expression that was nearly as soft as ever.

Father and son were in just this frieze two hours later when Vicki returned, her leaf-drenched car charging up the driveway past the gathering goblins. But by then Andrew knew that never, so long as he lived, never would he let a woman do such a thing to them again.

ENVY THE DEAD

Envy the dead. Janet MacArthur did. Every time the phone rang, she slammed down her shrimp-cocktail jar of rosé wine and got up from the chaise lounge with a grunt, skin suck-popping to the white plastic rungs, and waddled to the kitchen envying them. Perhaps she wouldn't have envied them so much if she had a phone extension out here by the pool, but no, her husband was too cheap for that. Put in an extension for *her*? You've got to be dreaming.

Or if it would be someone decent calling. But every damn time she smacked down her rosé wine and her literary magazine—hey, she was depressed, but there was no law against concrete poetry, was there?—and got up to take the call, it was another housewife on this godforsaken

Southern military base wanting a powwow, or one of her husband's Air Force friends pretending he had left his towel there and could he drop by to pick it up? Would now be okay? When no one's around and the skin is glistening with sweat beads so tasty you want to perch them on the tip of your tongue and close your eyes and *spin*? Janet MacArthur was *that* attractive to her husband's friends. But no, now was never a good time. She'd had it up to here.

The third time the phone rang on this particular overcast morning, partly sunny and partly overcast, Janet decided to let it be. Rot on the vine. Like the stringy creeper on her godforsaken trellis. Like the grass stubbing out in this drought. You call that *green*? Where she grew up, grass was *grass*. She watched a hornet sail by like a lazy death ship of the air. The white birdbath was dry again, she noted—how could it *not* be in weather like this? Looking at the empty birdbath always reminded Janet of one person coming without the other person. But the phone had a particular plaintive quality to it, like a calf with its head stuck inside a fence, getting periodic shocks from the electric current, and Janet banged down the magazine and rolled her devout fanny into the house. "Yah?" she said.

"Hello, Mrs. MacCarthur, this is a handicapped individual from Pride Products," the caller said. "We sell light bulbs made by epileptics—"

"Billy!" Janet MacCarthur screamed. "Billy, you bum. What are you doing calling all the way from San Jose?"

"No, no, lady, this is a handicapped individual," the caller said.

"This isn't my joker of a little brother Billy?"

"Uh-uh, sorry."

Janet flicked a sweat bead off the tip of her nose and turned on a sardonic smile that indicated she was envying the dead. "Go on," she said. "Let's hear it. What's wrong with you?"

"Most nearly anything you can think of, ma'am. Some of us are epileptics, some are amputees, though everyone is able to—"

"Nah; with *you*? What's wrong with *you*?" Janet demanded.

There was a slight cough on the other end, the audial equivalent of a blush. "In my case there seems to be a balance problem," the voice said. "My inner ear's screwed up."

"Billy!" screamed Janet. She was screaming with laughter. "Billy, if this isn't you. . . !" Suddenly Janet realized she sounded drunk, which she hardly was at all. She quieted down and said, "This is not Billy, right?"

"Right," said the caller. "I'm handicapped, from Pride Products. We sell key chains made by Speical Citizens, and things of this nature. I'd like to explain our goals to you, if you have a minute, Mrs. MacArthur, in the hopes that you can become one of our sympathetic supporters."

Very gingerly Janet laid the receiver down on the counter and tiptoed to the freezer for an ice cube. When she came back, the cube tucked inside one cheek, the caller was reaching the money part. Two dollars for every light bulb! Twelve dollars for every toothbrush! Bad enough to own a toothbrush with a specially thick handle, or some other feature to remind you each A.M. of the world's misfortunes, but twelve bucks! Janet cut the caller off.

"Honey, how'd you mess up that ear of yours?" she asked.

There was a silence. Janet played the question back to herself in her mind and it sounded perfectly sober to her. It was probably his shyness, then. She forged ahead.

"What was it, born that way?" she purred. "Vietnam?

Were you in the Nam, like my husband and a lot of other guys I know?"

"No, ma'am," said the caller hesitantly. "I couldn't get in because I already had the ear problem."

"Well, *tell* me, baby!" Janet insisted. She cracked the ice cube impatiently with her back teeth. "Tell your sweetheart 'cause your sweetheart wants to know," she sang, knowing that this did sound drunk, no question about it, but not caring a great deal. Who the hell cared. Janet was entitled to a little drinkey-drink of rosé wine in a camouflage glass at ten A.M. on days when she was envying the dead. Yah? Nah? Who the hell asked you? She would have done a dance step, as well, but it was too damn parched.

The caller told her a firecracker did it. He told her that when he was a youngster he'd gone to answer the door buzzer, put his eye to the peephole, and a firecracker went off inside the hole.

"What the hell's that got to do with your ear?" Janet shouted. "I mean I feel sorry for you and all, but what am I supposed to think when you tell me your ear—"

"My ear started to go bad after the eye went," the caller said.

"Now we're getting someplace," Janet said. "Okay, so we got a missing eye and a bum ear. Check. Any other little problem areas? Not to sound unconcerned with my fellow man's plight, but anything else?"

"I've got a frozen hip."

"*And* a frozen hip. Check," said Janet. "Okay. Where am I supposed to send my money?"

"This is not a charity, Mrs. MacCarthur," the caller said, after a dignified, perhaps even a cold, pause. "We're offering a range of products that can be of proven benefit to you in your kitchen, your bath, your laundry room—in fact, in every room in your house." There was another pause, of a different nature from the first. "This *is* a residence phone, is it not?" he asked.

"That it is," said Janet. Over the receiver, to the bowling trophy full of menu cut-outs, she whispered, "You . . . *got* to be dreaming."

"Then are we safe in assuming you are interested in prettifying your house, making it safer, more usable, and at the same time easier to keep up?"

"Hold this," said Janet. "Hold this right here." She put the phone on the counter, rolled out to her chaise, picked up her rosé and her journal and, blinking with the continual change of lighting, emptied the contents of the shrimp-cocktail jar into a fresh Dixie cup. She took up position atop the telephone stool. "Ready," she said. "Ready for the whole shooting match." She tilted her cup so the ice clinked back against her teeth.

"Pride Products," began the caller, "sells products made by persons incapacitated by handicaps major and minor. We sell light bulbs made by epileptics—"

"This is great," Janet said.

"—which carry a guarantee of two years except in cases where there's been obvious customer mishandling. Unlike other light bulbs which are manufactured on a conveyor belt, the epileptics who manufacture—"

"What's your name, honey?" Janet asked.

"My name?"

"You hear me jawing to anybody else?"

"T. Frederick Hunnibell," the caller said.

"Okay, Freddy," Janet purred. For some reason saying this name aloud made her feel like wiggling, right there on top of the telephone stool. "I am ready, Freddy!"

"Light bulbs. And key chains made by Spe——"

"Shoot to kill me, Freddy!" Janet shouted. "I am ready to go wherever you want to send me!"

There was a tiny click, and the line went dead.

Janet sat holding the receiver as if it were a dead weasel. Her face drained of color, she swallowed a teaspoon of heated oxygen, and when she closed her eyes the word *shame* lit up inside her brain, complete with floodlight and glitter.

————◇————

All the rest of the morning Janet sat by the pool in her white chaise lounge in a kind of morose stupefaction. If suicide didn't mean killing yourself, she thought, she would seriously consider committing suicide. She tried to nap but it was impossible—it was like watching her own funeral cortege get caught in a traffic jam. She watched the stunt planes from the airfield nearby as they darted upside down through the leaves of her mimosa tree, but she took no real enjoyment from them. (In fact, she looked the other way, knowing they were only some of her husband's friends showing off for her. What assholes. One time a handicapped guy came to one of *their* houses, she recalled, and the wife had called up to her husband in the privy, "Lieutenant, come on down here, what are you doing?" And the lieutentant had called down, just as sweetly as can be, "Having an orgasm." Selfish prick.) She fanned herself with her literary rag without getting any cooler. She drank from her Dixie cup without getting any drunker, feeling only crinkled and waxy-warm, like the cup. Her ear hurt, her eye hurt, and she did believe her hip felt frozen. She sat in a state of bewildered embarrassment, accepting the fact that for her and probably the whole damn Air Force, spiritual refreshment was out of the question; and envying the dead like mad.

Then the kitchen phone rang again. When she picked it up and T. Frederick Hunnibell began talking to her in that soothing dignified voice of his, Janet burst into tears.

"I am so sorry!" she burbled.

"No, it's I who am so sorry," Hunnibell said. "I've been trained to recognize many different kinds of customer reaction and I should have realized you were nervous. I shouldn't have hung up."

"Do a lot of people have trouble," Janet whimpered, "talking to handicapped guys?"

"Oh, heck yes." Hunnibell chuckled. Chuckling Hunnibell was a side she had never heard before. It made her feel so red-blooded again, she wanted to barbecue a T-bone right on the spot. She found herself wondering how old he was. "Orgasm" wasn't such an embarrassing word—it was embarrassing but in a kind of slithery fun way. She wondered why she was thinking that.

"I am also sorry," she said, "about being so free with your name."

"Listen, Mrs. MacArthur, I'm going to level with you," said Hunnibell. "My supervisor was listening in this morning, he was checking up on me you might say, and for acting so rude the way I did and hanging up on you I may just be out of a job unless you can see your way clear to help. Do you follow me?"

"I follow," said Janet. "I am so sorry! And I happen to need a light bulb for the basement . . ." Janet paused. The offer didn't seem significant enough. "And we're running out of key chains," she added nervously.

"I need to survey you," Hunnibell said distinctly.

"How's that?"

"Pride Products is always on the lookout for customer antagonism, though that's not what we'd call it in your case. We'd call it customer nervousness, but it falls under the same category. We want to know what makes you tick. We want to know, in short, what made you behave

183

the way you did on the phone with me earlier this morning. There are a few questions that could be of some help."

"Of course," said Janet, shaking her head so eagerly that a few drops of moisture spun off her hair tips and hit the fishing calender on the wall nearby. "Whatever I can do."

"Is now a good time?" Hunnibell asked.

"Fine."

"Could you give me directions, please? You're in Eisenhower South, aren't you, off Ulysses Grant Trail?"

"That's right," said Janet, taken aback, craning down suddenly at the sweat rivulet trickling between her bikini cups. "But does it have to be . . . in person?"

"Well, see," said Hunnibell in a slower, rather hurt tone. "All the best surveys are done in person, and I can assure you that the one I'll be bringing over is a very good one. It was drawn up by the Harvard Handicap Group, with a grant from Dr. Pepper. But if you'd rather not, or if today is a bad day . . ."

He was able to make it over in twenty minutes.

Janet heard the car pull up. She was practically dead sober now, but she pretended to be asleep in the white chaise lounge because it felt like the right thing to do. She heard Mr. Hunnibell calling "Mrs. MacArthur?" from the driveway, and then calling from the side, and there he was crunching up the white gravel path toward her right past the empty birdbath. Janet pretended to be awakening, ungluing herself from the white rungs, patting the back of one hand to a sticky brow, and looking up . . . at *him*. There he was, a bad eye for sure, and a weaving gait from either his frozen hip or his balance problem, but he was young—young like maybe twenty-two, and Janet hadn't conversed with anyone that young in a decade or more; since *she* was twenty-two.

"Mr. Hunnibell?" she asked.

"Hi, there," came the reply, and it was fabulous to put the voice together with this youthful figure, fabulous also to feel the former picture she had—of a rail-thin and old-before-its-time calf with gargoyle eyebrows—pull apart and shrivel to nothing like cotton candy in the sun. "You must be Mrs. MacArthur."

She kept her legs right where they were, looking lengthy on the chaise, hoping they would make him feel welcome. She wiggled her toes right up to her womb. "I must be," she said, looking up into the bomb of sunlight where he stood, and fixing her smile so it wouldn't come out squinty, "but I'm Janet."

In a second the young visitor had swept—arced—into the chaise lounge opposite. He gave her a very self-assured smile; a smirk, nearly. "Janet," he said, rolling the word from one side of his mouth to the other with enjoyment. "How come you're always on the winning team, Janet?" he asked.

"Huh?" said Janet. "Am I? How do you know?"

"Is it because that's the way your momma made you?" he asked.

For a second the stunt planes seemed like fleas to her, so near and insinuating they seemed. She felt like slapping the face of this smirking hunk sitting before her. "How old are you?" she demanded. "Twenty-two? Twenty-three? You ought to know better than to ask personal questions of older . . . ladies." She avoided using the word "woman" because it seemed too physical just at the moment. He surprised her. But then again, she liked surprises when they weren't too dangerous.

Hunnibell was taken aback. "I'm just a bag of hot air," he said, lowering his eyes and looking shyly at a crushed Fanta cup beneath her chaise. "I don't mean to be personal, and I'm sorry if it came out that way. I must be compensating again."

"For what?" Janet said, before she could stop herself.

They had another of their little silences. Kind of special, in a way. It wasn't every day you could have silences with someone you just met.

"I'm twenty-two," Hunnibell confirmed.

"I'm thirty-two," Janet said boldly, because why the hell not? Why make a secret of how long you've lived, for God's sake, especially when you were always surprising yourself so much you'd probably wake up the next day and be fifty, or fifteen again. You could wake up dead or alive, for all you knew. Crippled or insane. A dog. A pregnant parakeet. An Aztec god. Especially in heat like this. "Thirty-two, and I want a brew," she said, standing. "Can I grab you something from the fridge?" she asked her young guest.

"We're not supposed to drink on the job," Hunnibell said. They looked at each other till the last second before she entered the kitchen. "But I guess one beer would be all right," he added in time.

"I was about to have some salad; care to join me in some salad?" she called out, from the frosty space before the fridge that was so cold her nipples saluted smartly. There was no answer, or at least no answer she could hear. She threw some lettuce in two wood bowls with a slice of orange on each top, tried banging some California onion dressing on them but the bottle was empty, and started back. "Dream on," she murmured to herself, stopping. Then she yanked off her bikini top, popped an orange slice around each nipple, and with a sigh and a smile went on out to enjoy life.

SUMMER HEAT

In the summer heat the California bar was dark. Six or eight black hookers sat on stools in back, trying to keep cool. The bar owner was sitting and sweating through his clothes at the rearmost table as he tried to convince a black-bearded Hasid that he had come to the wrong place.

"No sir, no sir," said the Hasid, rapping the table.

"You're telling me you want to sleep with one of these women," said the bar owner.

"Yes sir," said the Hasid, staring at the olive-pit knees of the women as they pivoted on their stools and tittered.

"Holy shit," said the bar owner, mopping his head with a napkin as white and limp as the Hasid's clothes were black and stiff.

"It's a free country," the Hasid insisted.

"That's for sure," said the bar owner. He could think of nothing else to say.

With delicate steps in heavy shoes, the Hasid clopped his way to the end of the bar and inspected the faces of the hookers as best he could in the afternoon darkness. A tiny one in Adidas sneakers skipped out from the shadows across the room and said her name was Pearl and that she was fifteen.

"That's nice," said the Hasid, "but to put it frankly, that's a child, okeydoke?"

Pearl, blinking shyly, murmured that was okeydoke.

Turning, the Hasid's attention was caught by what looked for a second like a lighted aquarium over the bar—blue with large glowing goldfish swarming through—but which turned out, the next second, to be a color TV. He stood watching *Mod Squad* for a minute, fingering his payess, then with fierce dreaminess he faced the women again. They were all watching him. The bar owner had pushed out his chair and resumed penning "Shrmp Cktl: $4.95" on a stack of plastic menus. The Hasid clopped behind a woman who was neither prettier nor less pretty than her sisters, but who had a head of hair like a dark dandelion puff.

"That's Marguerite," said the bar owner without looking up.

The Hasid cupped Marguerite's breasts from behind and nearly pulled her off her stool.

"Watch it," she said. She said it laughing.

The girl with Adidas sneakers took a seat in front of *Mod Squad* and ordered a glass of pineapple juice.

The heat was bearable.

Marguerite led the stiff figure through the door in back and down a narrow sloping corridor painted a lemon-yellow so radiant it would have looked nuclear had it not become dingy with a film of dry lint that breathed with their passage. When they got to her room, the Hasid noticed a mezuzah on the doorway, corroded with age, but a mezuzah nonetheless. He asked her what was the name of the bar owner and she told him it was "Koch" and he asked her was he related to the mayor of New York and she told him, as she turned on the fan, that everyone is related somehow.

"Somehow or other," she said, yawning.

Marguerite was extremely black as she undressed on the bedsheets. Her belly was black and her breasts were black and her nipples were blacker.

"What brings you to sunny California?" she asked. "You're not from around here."

Letting one bricklike shoe hit the soft linoleum that was pocked with dozens of cigarette burns, the Hasid said he was from Brooklyn, New York.

"What brings you to sunny California?" she asked.

"Love," said the Hasid. "Love brings me to California. You're asking me, so I'm telling you. I'm looking for my two-year-old son that I love so much, when we both look in the mirror, it's only him I see."

"How'd he get lost?" she asked.

"His mother stole him away," the Hasid said, "after her boyfriend whipped his little head and threw him in a water wader so he nearly drowned."

Marguerite looked up at the Hasid as he slid about in his baby-white foot on the linoleum, removing his second black shoe.

"A water wader is a plastic tub," explained the Hasid. "You put water in it in the back hall and splash."

"What color was it?" was the only thing Marguerite could think to say.

"The water wader?"

189

"Yes."

"Rose, I think," said the Hasid. "Yes, I think, I think, rose, rose, I think. With Goofy and Donald Duck all up and down the sides."

Marguerite ran her fingernail along the seam of a patch that was starched into the sheet. She started to say something sympathetic, but "I know it, I know it," he said, interrupting her.

"Is the fan too noisy for you?" she asked.

"It's okeydoke."

"Do you want the light on or off?"

When he didn't answer, Marguerite reached out and clicked the light off.

There was breathing in the afternoon, and a song.

> *Summertime*
> *An' the livin' is easy*
> *Fish are jumpin'*
> *An' the cotton is high . . .*

Strains of the music kept seeping down slowly through the ceiling as they found a corner of coolness to pool together, away from the heat.

> *O yo' daddy's rich*
> *An' yo' momma's good lookin'*
> *So hush, little baby*
> *Don' you cry.*

"That's my favorite song," Marguerite admitted at one point, touching his shoulder blade.

The Hasid's eyes were blistered with tears as he lifted his face from the gray pillow and lightly kissed her nose. "Yah," he said. "I think, I think, mine too."

After the Hasid left, Marguerite lingered in her room a bit, running her fingernail along the seam of the patch in the sheet and looking through the fan to the swirling leaves of the maple tree in the alley outside. Through the moving blades of the fan the swirling leaves had an old-fashioned look, as of an old-time movie, and Marguerite saw clearly how each moment was passing, how each moment was spinning so quickly into the past that none of them belonged, in any real sense, to the present at all. She smelled the Hasid's sperm like the smell of boiled shrimp, and inspected herself for any signs of it coagulating on her black skin like bits of lemon pulp. She touched herself, the lips folded in on themselves like one of the Hasid's Brooklyn foods, like lox, bright-pink just darkening at the edges. *Their races could merge,* she thought. Then looked at half a green tennis ball in the sink. She pulled an expensive comb through her dark puff of hair. "Child, your head is going to seed," she told herself, pulling at the tangle.

The bar owner, Koch, thought he detected a look of vexedness on Marguerite's face when she returned to the bar from the lemon-yellow corridor. "If you're sorry for mankind, you can hit me," he told her.

Marguerite stood behind his chair and whacked him twice at the top of his spine.

SO LONG,
MILLION MILES

Gordon the Dane was hiking the mountain named Giant's Castle in the Drakensberg range two hundred kilometers south of Johannesburg, in South Africa, when he stumbled across the lovers. He hadn't seen a living soul for eight hours, since leaving his tent at six that morning; only dozens of red-rumped baboons screeching at him through the fog as they scampered to keep him from getting higher than they, a situation that made them feel imperiled, for some reason. Miraculous company! But more miraculous still were the spirits of Bushmen who used to live in these mountains and whose cave paintings could still be seen everywhere, festooning the cliffs like a secret code: They

193

were man; there was no mistaking the kinship. Though about noontime Gordon to his shame had violated whatever unspoken pact existed between himself and the Bushmen by vandalizing one of the paintings. With his sunglasses on to protect his delicate blue eyes against the blazing African fog, he had taken a stone, primitive tool for a primitive impulse, and chipped off the sepia likeness of an antelope to stick in his pocket. Whatever had made him give in to such acquisitiveness? Whatever had made him think his wife, at home in her antique shop in Copenhagen, would appreciate his offering? "Here, Bente," he could hear himself saying, "here's a piece of despoiled Africa for you. To make up for the fact I no longer love you."

It was less than five minutes after he had vandalized the Bushmen painting (and attracted their curse, likely), that he almost tripped over the lovers, lying peaceably on their backs in the middle of this deteriorated path; they'd been done awhile. "Hello," Gordon pronounced awkwardly, seeing them before they saw him. They were startled but they did not seem to mind so much being startled. "Hello," they easily answered, surely a most pleasant sound to hear after communing all morning with nothing but baboons and the legacy of long-dead Bushmen. And not only was the sound pleasant, the sight was, too—Gordon thought they were the most relaxed couple he'd ever seen. She was dressed skimpily in a loose white dress, and the dark hairs on her calves glistened like grass with whatever sunlight managed to pierce through the rolling fog. He was a soldier, half out of uniform—one of the tough South African commandos trained to hold back the tide of the Third World wherever it peeked out in this fat beefy country. (And God, was it: Businessmen bullied the highways with their BMWs, matrons charged you off the sidewalk with their sausage-swollen bellies.) But the soldier was obviously stoned. Therefore it was a given that he could not believe in his mission one hundred per cent. Such was the way it was with Gordon's generation; he had seen it so all over the globe. It was not that they would not have been startled to find themselves lose whatever cause they were engaged in, it's just that they wouldn't have minded so much being startled.

"How much longer till the rim?" Gordon asked.

"It winds along the top, on and on!" answered the boy in a way that made Gordon feel his question garish for being so un-stoned. Always interested in getting there, reaching the goal. Of course the trail went on and on!

"Tequila?" asked the boy, patting the ground between them, and half sitting up. "I'd offer grass but we've done it all."

"Where you from?" asked the girl, also reposefully sitting up, so Gordon could take an awkward seat on the soft cushion of decaying pine needles between them, and gingerly try a sip of tequila from the regulation South African Commando canteen.

"Denmark."

"Been here long?"

"In the country two weeks. In these mountains two days," Gordon answered. "But this is it; I'm catching a plane tonight."

"On business?"

"Jawling."

"Oh!" They laughed. Good word—it was Afrikaans for hang out, to take what comes.

"I got the word from a hitchhiker last week in Durban," Gordon pronounced. "I got a better phrase from another hitchhiker outside Johannesburg, when I asked her what the heap of slag was piled outside a gold mine, profiled

195

against the city. 'Mine dump' she told me, but I thought she was referring to the city itself—'*mind* dump.' Only later did I realize she wasn't making a political statement."

The boy and girl laughed pleasantly. The girl was focusing in on Gordon faster than the boy was; the boy's wits were elsewhere.

"'Mind dump,'" laughed the boy.

"That's what you get for picking up 'she' hitchhikers," said the girl. She wore a look of mock scolding. Then her face changed and she clucked with genuine concern. "But only two days here, that's a rushed jawl," she said.

"Well, I'm going other places after this," Gordon said.

"Oh? Where?" asked the girl.

"I'm having a bad time in my marriage," Gordon replied.

"I see," said the girl. It was all the place names she needed.

The boy took another sip of tequila. Ten meters above them, a baboon slipped out of the fog and moved behind a rock.

"Maybe when I get back it will be better," Gordon told the girl, leaning back on his elbows and trying to affect the same calm they had.

"I hope so," said the girl. She smiled, too, airy and heartfelt at the same time.

"So what have you concluded?" asked the boy, the soldier, in a quiet, nonaggressive way. "Have you concluded we're all a bunch of red-meat-eating fascists?"

"Some," Gordon admitted. "The older generation, mostly. Every restaurant I go in, they're stuffing their faces with chops, steaks . . ."

They knew what he meant.

"Finally I asked a colored hitchhiker, that same one who told me about 'mind dump,' and you know what she said?"

The soldier smiled. "We're carnivores."

"Exactly," Gordon said. He was surprised. And because of the kindship he felt at that moment, Gordon felt caressed with human understanding. How relaxing just to come across such intimate human contact on a foggy mountain path. At a bus stop in a city, they all would have kept their distance. But here they were family—his blood brother, his blood sister. With the insulted air of being left out, the baboon above them tossed a stone that fell ludicrously short.

"Did you sleep with her?" asked the girl. "The colored hitchhiker?"

Gordon paused, feeling both sets of eyes on him in mild curiosity. He felt safe that they were not judging him. He nodded. "Audrey," he said.

"Good name," they both agreed. They laughed warmly. "Good name."

"I never slept with a colored woman before," Gordon confessed. "I never even particularly wanted to. But in this country, I wanted to."

The boy raised his eyebrows in assent. Of course it was technically part of his job to arrest people who sexually crossed the color line. He handed the tequila bottle to Gordon.

The girl was staring at Gordon's pale cuticles.

"Are you sleeping with everybody?" she asked.

Gordon shrugged. "Not everybody," he said.

"Did you draw blood?" the girl asked. "It's only real if you draw blood."

"African pigs!" Gordon said.

"We're carnivores!" the girl laughed. She reached forward and with kindness rubbed Gordon's arm, and squeezed his elbow.

"Well," Gordon said. He was thinking, shyly, of the way he had wanted to kiss Audrey good night, in the lobby of the hotel he'd brought her to, and never mind that all the white bellboys would be snickering. It was the gesture he wanted to make—not a political kiss but one of human beings abetting each other. Drawing blood would have been furthest from his mind. But he'd run to a telephone instead.

"In fact I called my wife right afterward," Gordon confessed. "I knew what I wanted to say. I wanted to say how much sleeping with someone else made me miss her, going halfway around the world to find someone illegal to sleep with made me love her almost enough."

He took the tequila bottle from the boy. "But I guess I woke her up. She takes a nap in the early evening. And I knew the last thing she wanted was me to foist any more ambivalence on her. So we had nothing to say to each other. It was a terrible connection anyway." He tried another sip. "But that's the way it's been for months, even when we're together in the same room. Static and echoes. So finally we said nothing. For about forty seconds: all that ocean and air between us. And I hung up."

The boy and girl waited.

"'So long, million miles,'" I said, and then I hung up. It was over."

"The curtain falls!" the girl said. She was only half mocking him.

Just at that time, about twenty-eight drops of rain fell out of the fog—materialized from the air—and stopped again. The baboon plunged out from the rock ten meters away and staggered up the hill until her red rump patch was lost in the fog. Gordon stared at where the red had been.

"It's to attract the males," the girl said.

"I know," Gordon said. "It's just . . . so pushy!"

They laughed. Then the girl said, "Oh, stop acting so vegetarian!"

"Am I acting vegetarian?" Gordon said in surprise. Then he threw his shoulders back and flashed her a jaunty, Scandinavian smile. It showed a good Nordic set of teeth, but still he felt a sissy somehow, so lily-white and untested next to these rugged South Africans.

"You don't have to pretend," the girl said with a level gaze.

"Well, now you've embarrassed me," Gordon said. "I don't mean to give you only one side of the picture."

"You don't have to be embarrassed," the girl said.

"Maybe we'll still work it out," Gordon said. "I don't want you to think we might not work it out."

"Well, it's an adventure, anyway," the girl said.

"What—falling out of love?"

"Sure," said the girl. "Why not? Even that."

"I don't know if I can do that," Gordon said, shaking his blond head skeptically.

"You could if you got back your blood lust," the girl said.

The boy took a sip of tequila for himself and held on to the bottle.

"Well," Gordon said, and just at that moment, the girl reached forward and took hold not of his arm again, but of his chin. "Here's some of it back," she said, and kissed him so hard that her teeth touched through his lip. A bite! A drop of crimson he could taste!

"You two going to make love?" the soldier asked good-naturedly. "I'll just push on into those bushes yonder, if you'd rather I didn't watch."

From somewhere, a baboon screeched.

The girl was leaning over Gordon to take off his sunglasses. "I have to see what your eyes look like, you northern peach—"

"We're not going to do this!" Gordon shrieked. His tongue was dry. He was afraid.

The girl and boy looked at him startled for a moment, but not minding so much being startled. Then, in weary concert, and with two almost inaudible sighs, they lowered themselves to the path again, lying there on either side of him. They squinted up through the fog to where the light was brightest, wearing wandering half-smiles.

"I've got to go," Gordon begged, tasting the blood. "My plane . . ."

They said nothing, pleasantly soaking up the fog with half-smiles into the sky. "Suit yourself," their smiles said. "Don't worry about anything." "Don't get lost in any mind dumps." And also, most of all, since he had no use for them and therefore they had no further use for him, "Ciao." The international noncommital word.

Gordon leapt awkwardly to his feet. Feeling almost supernaturally virginal in his unstoned panic, he patted his pockets to see what he'd left. "Ciao," he said.

Gordon descended the path in the fog. It was easier coming down than going up, though the pressure on the downside of his shoes grew with every hundred steps. Liberated from them, and from his wife, his coordination was off, as though he'd lost his bearings. He felt homeless, without a stick of shelter anywhere in case animals screeched at him through his descent, in case Bushmen communed. He felt bereft, as though it were violently wrong-headed of him to have rejected the lovers. They were offering companionship, the kindness of simple human company, and he'd flinched by instinct, turning his back. He felt heartless, as though falling out of love with one human being had made him incapable of taking solace from any others. For the first time, Gordon felt how risky the adventure of divorce would be, to be so cut off, to keep his wants to himself. Gordon kept climbing down, with the continual taste of blood on his lip. When eventually he spotted his camp far below, he had to take off his shades to double-check that what he was seeing was correct: A group of baboons was shredding his tent, covering the canvas with rocks. Gordon flung his cave-painting fragment at them, shrieking oaths as he charged.

ARTURO AND EVE

The father of the bride—an Italian widower, from Florence—is pacing on the wooden deck in southern California. Back and forth, before the ceremony—back and forth. Why did Arturo Casiglio's daughter have to be married in the bizarre American land of southern California? But never mind, never mind, losing a daughter would be difficult anywhere. Beneath the deck, someone in preparation clicks off a tape recording of "Figaro," speeds it forward, clicks it on, clicks it off, speeds it backward, clicks it on. Arturo Casiglio is frowning as he paces on the deck in his double-breasted black suit. He feels breathlessly formal, out of place. He speaks no English; the "Figaro" is like an old friend and he would hum it, but there is the incessant winding and rewinding of the tape.

America, he swears. He taps the miniaturized video camera in his pocket (not yet realizing it is empty of tape; the
ceremony will go up like smoke, unrecorded). Arturo Casiglio is alone on the deck, but whenever any of the easygoing American wedding guests lopes through the sliding
glass doors to join him for a moment, he pumps the person's arm, nodding and smiling with his lack of speech,
fluttering his hand against his heart to indicate his state,
and saying, *"Prima, prima."* Eve is the first of his children to
marry. Would he, for his four sons, fly from Florence to
this wilderness of southern California? He does not know.
He only knows he would do it for Eve. He would fly under
his own power, flapping his arms across the oceans. On
the spot, he would compose "Figaro" and sing all the parts
at once. It has to do with her dark-red hair.

———◇———

Arturo Casiglio has rented a castle in the mountains to
the north of Florence. The idea is for the family to con-
gregate here, to reunite. A summer holiday—it has been
too long. It is not gruesome to him that the factory no
longer requires his actual presence, that it is sufficient that
he can be reached by telephone if there is a question about
a certain glaze, a certain tile; that all summer the telephone is silent. It is not gruesome that all summer the four
sons not two hundred miles away do not trouble themselves to make the trip, to reunite. What is gruesome to
Arturo Casiglio is that Eve—*prima!*—has not come. All
summer the father curses the daughter. He fires off wither-
ing letters, snapping like vultures through the skies. He
wants to kill her. What is she trying to do to him? The
letters grow soft as doves. He loves her too much. Is she
going to let herself grow strange, this dear girl? On the last
day of summer there is a gray moth in the turreted window
of the castle, which Arturo Casiglio all alone has deter-

mined to capture with his handkerchief and set free out-of-doors. Approaching it, he sees it is not gray at all but red, dark red inside like her hair when it flutters its wings against the leaded glass.

———◇———

The four sons and one daughter exchange letters about their father. He is not well. But he has not been well for a long time. Ah, but this is different. He cries at the drop of a hat. He cries to see a little girl in a cap at the drugstore. What is wrong, the letters ask—is it his old grief for our mother? No no, this is different. For what, then? The letters shake their heads, flitting across the Alps, across the ocean, filling the sky like pale seabirds. There is no reason for his tears, the letters decide. Therefore there is nothing to be done about them, the letters agree. Somewhere in the air the letters shrug their shoulders, and turn to other matters. However, there is one last letter on the subject, an inquiry from Eve with her American family in southern California. What color was the cap? After a puzzled silence the answer comes back: dark red. Why did I ask that? Eve's next letter asks—I don't know why I asked that.

———◇———

Eve understands she must come home. He is the only father she has, and he is in a coma. The question is: When should she come home? What if he is in a coma for days and weeks? How can Eve leave her strong American husband and her strong American twin boys in the wilderness of southern California for what could turn out to be a long and useless time? Is it not furthermore true that he is, after all, in a coma that smells like old bacon boxes in the cellar and that he would not know the difference whether she comes home or not? So Eve waits. It is a lucky thing, she decides, that she chose to do so. Arturo Casiglio is in a coma for nine months. When he astounds the doctors by coming out of it, the doctors assure everyone there will be ferocious brain damage at the best. Meanwhile Eve has problems in other areas. Her twin boys have run away to a religious training camp in the foothills of Nepal. They are looking for the origins of man, their letters say with a sigh. It is hopeless, they say, but they are looking.

———◇———

Arturo Casiglio's four sons, Eve's brothers, have all been killed in a fishing accident. The boat they had chartered for the afternoon was exploded by a political faction. Arturo Casiglio does not care. Since his coma he has been making a recovery that is wonderful in its physical aspect, deplorable in its emotional one. Arturo Casiglio no longer cries. Instead, he laughs. Anything makes him laugh. On the day they told him about his four sons he stood outside his tile factory and made fun of the passing children, raising his leg like a dog going pee. Eve's letters scorch the sky, demanding an explanation from the doctors. Her letters go unanswered. At home in southern California, she wails that it is cruel for nature to play such a joke on a dignified old man. Actually it is common as dust, as the doctors know.

———◇———

Eve has tried too hard to come home for the funeral of her four brothers, as she tried too hard to come home for her father's old coma. Again it has taken too much out of her. In the southern California shopping mall two miles from her ranch house the dressmaker whispers to the hairdresser that Eve has put on weight. She has put on worry lines. Poor thing, they say—she wanted to go but what kind of funeral would it be when they had no remains of the bodies? When there were not even remains of the boat? Italian politics, swear the merchants of the southern California shopping mall. Adds the travel agent: Nevertheless she ought to have gone. Think how far up the creek I'd be if everyone canceled their plans just on account of a few marital problems.

———◇———

Arturo Casiglio has purchased for himself the castle in the mountains to the north of Florence. He lives there like a hermit, chasing to set free the numerous gray moths which are dark red on the inside. In his mind the "Figaro" is clicking forward, rewinding back; in his eyes is a look as if the tape is missing.

There one day is the long-delayed reunion with his daughter. She stops in after her divorce; she is on her way to Australia, where her sons are said to be going aboriginal. Parents chasing their children, she tells her father with a bitter laugh, but both the bitterness and the laughter fade slowly when she hears no echo from him.

They sit and sit.

Outside the castle, the sky is filled with the letters of other families, letters crying, letters beseeching, letters of misjudged feelings and lapsed passions and mystery and regret and hope. Now slowly at last these pale birds are resting their wings. The sky is becoming clear once more as all correspondence fails and enduring emptiness suffuses the world. Nothingness fills the wind: the very molecules of the air hum with it, the bones in people's skulls resonate with nothingness as if with influenza, a flu of nothingness, like radio waves of silence. Memories die. Already in the room of the ancient castle where Arturo and Eve sit, eternity is cresting the ozone as both remember less and less, and finally not at all, the time decades ago when they had walked together in the park in Florence, a young red-haired girl hand in hand with her dashing young father, and she was asking Why is this tree here? Why is this hill? Pappa, oh Pappa, can we be friends forever?

THE ESCARGOT STORY
(THE STROKE, II)

Such a long time ago that it was only with difficulty recalled, but then recalled vividly—it was only eight
years!—Lucas had loved a girl in college. The girl's name
was Caroline Deerfelt, and she had a father who had suffered a stroke that had partially paralyzed him, and, life
being the way it is, the stroke had partially paralyzed Caroline, too. Caroline tried with all her might not to let it
paralyze her, but in the end it did, and the love she felt for
Lucas seized up into a spasm she would not allow Lucas to
try to soothe; yet though it was not possible for Caroline
and Lucas to be together and they went their separate
ways, they remained alive for each other, so that each of
them in their separate cities, every so often, would pick up

a book that had the other's name in it, and each would fall into a commotion of yearning that was as impossible to fix as it was quiet.

Lucas married Caroline's best friend and they had two boys and they were extremely happy. "Do you realize we're living happily ever after?" Lucas asked his wife once, and by way of answer she had smiled back a smile so innocent that Lucas had inexplicably smelled with it the chilly scent of guilt. Life being the way it is, they had no communication with Caroline or her father, hearing only that Caroline was unhappy and adrift, wandering from Providence to Wyoming to Washington, D.C., and that Mr. Deerfelt had moved out of Manhattan and gone back to Buffalo, where he had been raised and had raised Caroline, where his heart belonged (he and Caroline used to describe the city with such nostalgia that Lucas had come to envision it as a romantic fur-trading outpost, grown up to have its boulevards lined with elm trees), and where life could be expected to be more genteel, taken all around, on a man with half the weight of his body dead. The subject of Caroline and her father came up frequently in the beginning of Lucas' marriage to Caroline's best friend, but as the boys came along and filled out their lives it came up less and less, though it was always there in the background, like the sound of birds starving.

Lucas and Wanda had money—having inherited it from people they ardently wished had not died—and one of the things they did with their money was vacation, each summer, in northern Ontario, driving up from Providence, across the Berkshires, across New York State, up from Buffalo past Niagara Falls and into Ontario. Lucas, especially, loved the drive. Far better than a runner's high, to his way of thinking, was a driver's high, which could be gotten only by staying at the wheel and racking up three, four, five hundred miles; against the lovely sounds of his wife comforting his two boys, his mind would come unhinged and he would build great sand castles of thoughts, washing them away and building new ones, figuring out his life and the lives of his family, and remembering.

Coming home from Ontario at the end of one summer, the last summer before he turned thirty, Lucas let himself remember Mr. Deerfelt. All afternoon it rained, and they were stuck on one of Ontario's back roads behind a cabbage truck, and they were listening to a classical music station that was playing, he was almost sure, Lucas' aunt, a harpsichordist. The boys were crying in the back seat, and his wife was twisted around to comfort them, and all Lucas had to do the entire afternoon was keep an eye on the road—make sure no cabbages rolled off the truck onto them, that was all; and periodically decline the egg-salad sandwich offered him by his wife—so that Lucas in a lengthy paroxysm of happiness and security felt free in a way he hadn't felt free in years to remember Mr. Deerfelt, the watery hulk of him propped in a chair, talking and talking about the things he loved in the world. And there were only three! Three things he loved, in all the world! Over and over from his position in his stiff ladder-back chair the stroke victim would name them: Caroline, first and foremost, and, fathers and daughters being what they are, least possible for him to keep; his oboe, which had seemed to shrink in its case, to atrophy, after his stroke, till there seemed so little point in keeping it that he'd sold it to supplement his welfare payments; and escargots.

Escargots. How Mr. Deerfelt would talk himself silly about escargots, sprinkled with parsley and shallots, escargots drowned in lemon juice with mushrooms. Shaking

himself from his stiff lethargy, his huge pink eyes shower-
ing sparks, Mr. Deerfelt would rhapsodize about escargots,
his good hand rising from the tabletop to describe the
aroma, to describe the taste; his bad hand nearly levitat-
ing, too, with all the excitement he was talking up. But of
course Mr. Deerfelt was poor, and he had no money to
throw away on a $5.95 hors d'oeuvre. It had been years
and years since his tongue had touched escargots, dripping
in hot garlic butter, although he had such a great time
talking about them, he almost didn't seem to realize any
time had passed at all.

If only the past could be purchased! Lucas thought, as
he sometimes did, on his dreary, dreamy drives. Couldn't
their money be used to buy it back, a little bit—to buy a
present for someone who'd featured in their past, and
who'd never expect it? Lucas and Wanda had sometimes
tried to do exactly that—to go out and buy something for
someone from the long ago: a new coat, once, for an old
dancing teacher who the papers said had been mugged;
cash, once, for an old swimming coach whose house had
burned. Lucas and Wanda tried not to feel confused about
how they happened to be in a position to give—they just
gave, anonymously—and every time they did they felt
connected in an almost spooky way—their past and present welded together—until the future happened by in its
careening, broken-footed way.

As the rain let up, and the radio announcer announced
that it had been someone other than Lucas' aunt playing
Scarlatti all afternoon, and they turned past the cabbage
truck onto the expressway at last for Buffalo, Lucas imagined that one of the finest things he could do, as an adult
who loved his past, was to buy some escargots for Mr.
Deerfelt.

It was the midpoint of the journey, and instead of checking into one of the Holiday Inns ringing Buffalo, as they usually did, Lucas got off the highway and ventured for the first time into the fur-trading outpost of the city that had nurtured both the girl who'd nearly become his wife, and the man who'd nearly become his father-in-law. Not unexpectedly—his curiosity accustomed to bending in on itself in a hurry—billboards advertising dog food filled the sky as soon as he came off the ramp, and he drove with lowered gaze through a downtown that was deserted, denuded . . . Buffalo having lost some of its population as well as all its elm trees in the last decades . . . until he located the Statler, looking the way grand old hotels do when they are no longer grand. They parked, then tramped through the empty lobby under a chandelier that looked ready to drop upon the royal-blue carpet curling around its edges, took two adjoining rooms on the eleventh floor, and called down for a "deviled-egg plate," although Lucas had no appetite for anything. Three times the three-year-old wanted to find the ice machine, so Lucas took him out the door and down the hall three times. It was a very big and clunky ice machine with a noise so frightening to the three-year-old that he could not keep away from it.

At last, it having grown dark and an intrusive klieg light begun flashing past their windows, advertising the debilitated hotel, Lucas flopped on one of the beds with the Buffalo phone book, and found Deerfelt, Aaron. So there he was again! The past fetched back in an instant! Lucas was stunned that it was so easy to go back so far.

"What's the matter? You look like you just saw a ghost," Wanda said.

It always surprised Lucas how un-self-absorbed his wife

could be when she was nursing the baby, and he sighed and looked stern. Then he laughed and said, "I just had an idea. I don't know if it's a good idea, or what."

"Tell."

"Oh, it's stupid, probably. It doesn't make sense. I was just thinking on the way in here that Buffalo is where Caroline's father resettled, remember? After leaving New York? I don't know who told us, about five or six years ago?"

"Graham."

"Graham, yeah, that's right. I don't know how he found out."

"He ran into Caroline at O'Hare."

Lucas watched his wife switch the baby to her other breast. Her knees were crossed elegantly as she sat on the edge of the bed. The music of a *Roadrunner* cartoon chase drifted in from the TV in the other room, where the three-year-old sat transfixed.

"Such a long time ago," Lucas said.

Wanda looked up at Lucas and smiled dimly.

"What do you want to do," she said—"all of us pay him a visit?"

"If it's going to upset you we don't have to do anything," Lucas said.

"I'm not upset!" Wanda said innocently. "I used to have my own relationship with Mr. Deerfelt, don't forget. We used to like each other quite a bit. I wouldn't mind seeing him again. I just think it would be . . . strange, that's all."

"I'm not talking about seeing him."

"What *are* you talking about?"

"Sending him some escargots. Anonymously."

Wanda looked down at the baby at her breast. The baby was asleep, his cheeks placid. Wanda tickled him expertly in the roll of fat under the pointed barb of his chin, and his cheeks began pumping again like tiny pistons.

"I think that's a beautiful idea," Wanda said.

Now it was Lucas who was unsure. "You don't think that would connect us again, somehow, with Caroline?"

"Not if we don't want it to," Wanda said evenly.

That, then, was that (it had to be). But first the great crowd of family details needed their nightly tending. Midway through the TV-extracting and hands-washing and dinner-eating (they called the deviled eggs dinner, since Lucas still had no appetite) and the scolding and crying and sudden hugging that constituted the wealth of family life, and that Lucas knew he loved, Lucas got fed up.

"I'm going down to the bar," he announced.

Wanda looked at him with a boy at each shoulder. "Thanks a lot," she said.

"Why should I pay six bucks for a drink by room service when I can go right downstairs and have it for four?"

"What do you need a drink for at all? Why just now?"

Lucas felt as friendless and as leafless as downtown Buffalo. He put his fingertips to his thinning hair. "Well, wait," he said. "Just stop right there. Most of the times I don't, and some of the times I do. And that's my right."

"See you tomorrow," Wanda said.

"See you tomorrow," the three-year-old echoed.

"See you in about forty-five minutes," Lucas said. "Bolt the door after me."

On his way out the door he saw Wanda drop to her knee to catch one of the soft yellow eggs that was leaping away from her, but he took a breath against that part of his chest that wanted to rush back in and catch it for her.

———◇———

The bar was crowded. It was, the out-of-towner realized, Friday night; the new-styled Statler bar seemed to be not so much a place where fur-trappers romanced and roughhoused in the grand tradition as a place where low-

215

ranking chemical-company executives took the secretary pool to flirt. Lucas took a seat at the left center of the horseshoe-shaped bar, next to five noisy older men standing around one noisy older woman who was telling an off-color joke—something about a samurai swordsman castrating a housefly—and he turned his attention to a large TV with the sound off until the bartender approached.

"What'll it be?" asked the bartender, as glum and impassive as the TV talk-show guest, whose face was being slowly squirted with whipped cream by the uproarious talk-show host.

"Just a shot, I guess. Jack Daniels. You know what time it is?"

Impassively the bartender, passing the electronic cash register beneath his TV, pressed a button that caused the numbers 814 to flash up, in green. It stayed that way for a moment, and then 814 turned to 815.

"Huh," said Lucas, at 816, when the bartender returned. Then: "Aren't there any girls around this place?"

"Girls?" asked the bartender, scowling.

"Yeah. You know."

The bartender chuckled miserably as he put the napkin down, and turned away.

Lucas left him a tip, drank his shot, and inspected the rug, which looked as though it had suffered a flood, and fiddled with a crocus in a dish on the bar, until the bartender returned.

"Another?"

"Nah, forget it," Lucas said, changing the subject. He stuck the crocus in his lapel, feeling good from the drink: encapsulated in protein. "Didn't this city used to be kind of—"

"Kind of what?" the bartender interrupted.

"I don't know: more splendid?"

The bartender flicked a glance at him then, his first glance, and took his shot glass, and replaced it with a new one that was filled to the rim. "This one's on the house," he said, sliding away again.

As 818 turned to 819, and the impassive talk-show guest began his turn of impassively squirting the uproarious talk-show host, the bartender came by with a half-smoked cigarette, and he put the cigarette in an ashtray in front of Lucas. "Girls, huh?" he asked.

"No, never mind," Lucas said.

"Well, don't give up the chase quite yet. Around ten there might be a girl or two coming by."

Lucas considered. "Guests aren't allowed to take bar drinks up to their rooms, are they?"

"Sure thing."

"They are?"

"Sure thing."

"In that case, could I have a double to take up?" Lucas said.

"Sure. And around ten I could send up someone with *another* double," the bartender suggested with a leer.

"To tell you the truth, and you have my apology for it, but I was just curious about the procedure, was all," Lucas said, standing up and taking out his wallet to tip him again. "I never would've had the nerve to ask if I didn't have my whole family upstairs."

The bartender choked on his cigarette, and fetched him a double.

Wanda was surprised to be unbolting the door for Lucas so soon.

"I missed you," Lucas explained, looking up at her as he leaned in the doorway, sipping.

Wanda blushed, squeezed his hand, and turned to walk down the hall into the bedroom, saying "Be careful" to the three-year-old, who had a mouth full of sponge cake.

"Don't choke," Lucas echoed, following her.

"Rrr, rrr," barked the three-year-old, turning the pages of a dog book.

On the bed like an embroidered engine, like some perpetual-motion machine in Doctor Denton's, the baby lay snapping his limbs, his lips bubbling with concentration.

"What did you decide?" Wanda asked.

"About what?"

Wanda sat on the bed next to the phone book.

"Oh, about Mr. Deerfelt?" Lucas asked airily. "I don't know. I don't think so. Why shake up a hornet's nest? Besides," he said, "I doubt there's a restaurant willing to, you know, send out escargots. It's crazy."

Wanda said, "I think I found one that's likely."

"You *what?*"

Wanda stared back at him. "What's the matter?" she asked.

Lucas felt rushed and confused, drained by her benevolence. "Well, I mean, the best bet would be the restaurant right here in this hotel, wouldn't it?"

"They already told me they've never heard of snails," Wanda said without rancor, flipping over the Yellow Pages right next to the baby's head. "Here it is," she said, turning the book around.

Lucas blinked at a quarter-page ad for a French restaurant, located just numbers away from Mr. Deerfelt's address off Gates Circle. The ad showed a maître d' with a goatee puckering his lips and saying, "We deliver."

"You really want to do this?" Lucas asked.

"Only if you do," Wanda said. "I think Mr. Deerfelt would be thrilled out of his mind."

The onslaught of so much trust gave Lucas a sudden urge to rinse his hands. He walked into the bathroom and put his glass on the glass shelf above the sink, and filled the sink with cold water, and sank his fists in it. He opened his hands underwater, and raised his fingertips to his eyes in the mirror, where they dripped as he looked at himself with a puzzled expression. Then he took the glass out and put it by the telephone on the bedstand, and he sat down.

"I'm calling his apartment first," he said. "I'm going to make sure he's home."

"Good idea," Wanda said.

"I'm not going to talk to him, I'm just going to make sure he's home."

"Good," Wanda said, brushing crumbs of sponge cake from around the mouth of the three-year-old, and blowing them out from between the pages of his book.

Lucas dialed the number, turned white, and slowly hung up the phone.

"What is it?"

Lucas swallowed. "It was a young woman's voice. A young woman answered.

"Caroline?"

"No, no. For a second I thought so, but it wasn't Caroline. I think there was an accent."

"How is that possible? Who could it be? He never had any young friends, did he? Certainly no young women friends?"

Wanda and Lucas looked at each other with fright for a second, the past zooming in low over their heads like bomber planes, and then Lucas got control of the situation.

"Oh," he said, feeling infinitely relieved. "It was a housecleaner! Someone probably who comes in for an hour once a week."

"Or a part-time nurse," Wanda agreed. "His health is probably more fragile than ever."

"Of course! But still—I'm not going to order escargots for him unless I'm certain he's home."

"Um," Wanda said.

"My idea, really, was to order out a super portion, and candles and a tablecloth and silver, too. I'd like to do it up right, as long as we're doing it—but I'm not going to do it if he's out at a movie somewhere."

"Why don't you call the restaurant first and find out if they'll *do* all that?"

"They'll do it, if we let them name their price."

They thought, in silence that had the slight sour smell of dollar bills to it, about how true that was.

"Well, it was a nice idea."

"That's it?" Wanda asked. "It's over?"

"What else can I do?"

"You can call his apartment and simply ask if he's there."

"Oh," Lucas said. "Life doesn't have to be so complicated?"

Wanda smiled, showing her pretty teeth, because her husband appeared good to her, her husband appeared generous. "Lucky," she said. It was his old nickname, hardly ever used anymore.

But now the boys were falling asleep. The baby had stopped snapping his limbs and bubbling; now only his cheeks were working with a dream of milk. The three-year-old was nodding off with his thumb in his mouth.

"Hey," Lucas said, gently shaking him. "I want you awake for a while, and nice and tired in the car tomorrow."

"Rrr," came the boy's soft bark of protest. And his eyes closed.

They looked at him.

"How do you want to arrange tonight's sleeping?" Lucas asked. "You want to sleep in here with the baby, and I'll take this one in the other room with me?"

"What would you like to do?"

"Well, that way I could get a good night's sleep before the drive tomorrow. If you're going to have to get up to nurse the baby anyway."

"You're not just *dying* to sleep with me tonight?" Wanda teased him.

Lucas took it seriously. "Well, I do get to sleep with you every night," he said.

"I'm *kidding*," Wanda said.

"It's not like I ever get a chance to miss you. I'm with you every single day and every single night. I mean I have to scrape and bow just to get away to a bar for a few minutes."

"Take it *easy*," Wanda smiled, holding up the remains of the deviled-egg plate. "Here, are you hungry? You didn't have anything to eat. What's the *matter*?"

Lucas sat stiff on the faded bedspread. "I'm not hungry! I'm talking about sleeping in a separate bed for one night!" he said.

"Absence makes the heart grow fonder. I *know*," Wanda laughed. "What're you getting so upset about?"

For only a minute longer did Lucas sit rigid. Then he exhaled, letting his muscles loose. He slumped. "I'm just exhausted," he said. He closed his eyes for a minute; then got up with much creaking of the bed that sounded to Lucas like the creaking of his own joints, and carried the three-year-old to one of the two beds in the adjoining room, where he laid him out and stripped him and pressed the inert stately limbs into the proper pajama holes. He lay in the dark on his own bed, toying with the crocus

very lightly, and watched the klieg light veer past his window; lighting up the separate rooms where two children
lay separately, on their separate beds, and two adults, also,
lying separately with their shoes on.

In a minute Lucas had picked up the phone in his room
and was dialing the numbers again.

"Hello?" said the slightly wary voice with the accent.

"Hello," Lucas said. "Is Aaron there, please?"

"Aaron?" asked the voice.

"Yes. Is he there?"

A pause.

"No . . ."

"Aaron Deerfelt? It says in the phone book that this is
his number?"

"No, he is not here. I think, I think . . . he is dead. He
died two years ago."

"Dead!"

"I am sorry."

"Dead?"

Wanda appeared in the doorway, framed by light as if
by shock and grief, nodding with her hand at her mouth.

"Dead," Lucas said softly.

Wanda nodded again, and said, "Ah!"

"I had no *idea,*" Lucas told the voice. "I haven't seen him
in many years. Since before he moved out of New York, in
fact. I'm so sorry."

"I am so sorry to *tell* you," said the voice. It was a shy
and unaffected voice, but lilting.

"How did he die?"

"This I don't know precisely. I am only here the last
year."

"You didn't know him?"

"No, I never had the privilege to meet him. I am a niece
of his wife's."

"His wife's!?"

"Yes. You do not know he got remarried? Oh, yes, five years ago it would be in November. I have her number if you would like to call, I am sure she would be most unhappy if I told her you called and she missed you. Or perhaps you would not . . ."

"He got remarried," Lucas told Wanda, who almost tripped with surprise into the room, then turned on tiptoe into her room and came back to give Lucas his bourbon glass.

"Yes, she moved out, and I have been living here temporarily only this one year," the voice was saying. "You were . . . very good friends?"

"Good acquaintances," Lucas found himself saying, and drained the glass.

"You are a musician, also?"

"No . . . no. Are you?"

"Yes. I am a violinist. I am just over from Warsaw this one year."

"Oh? With the symphony?"

"Yes. And . . . and the University here."

Lucas took his wife's hand and pressed it to his cheek. He had nothing to say. He was thinking that the voice sounded like a violin. Then he said, "What is your name?"

A pause.

"Veronica. And yours?"

A pause.

"Lucas."

"Hello, Lucas."

"Hello, Veronica."

"This must be a terrible sadness."

Lucas did not say anything.

"I do understand, I think," Veronica said. "You go away, and things break."

"That's right," Lucas said.

"There are cracks everywhere, and in all things," Veronica said.

"That's right," Lucas said. "In every painting. In every piece of music . . ."

"And in every friendship, in every affair of the heart . . ."

"Cracks for people to fall through."

"Precisely. I do understand."

"I know it, Veronica. I know that you do. . . ."

Reluctantly they said good night to each other, and the violin voice proceeded to fill Lucas' head as he stood holding Wanda for a little while in the sad quiet of their hotel room. Neither of them cried. "You didn't ask about Caroline," Wanda said after a while.

And after another while Lucas replied, "I didn't want to know."

Soon Wanda went to her room. Lucas lay on his bed with the beautiful violin voice filling his head in the reeling darkness. Whenever he closed his eyes he felt the motion of the car, the shudder and speed of the road. He knew in his body the obsession everything had to speed behind him and fall away, and there was something else his body knew, as well, something else he recognized—the sound of birds starving, thousands of them crying out with broken tongues as they flooded past all sides of him in the reeling darkness . . . And then out of the reeling darkness, the violin voice and the voices of birds were interrupted by a new voice.

"Was that the lady with the accident?"

"What?"

"The lady with the accident?" the three-year-old repeated.

"Oh—no. The lady with the *accent,*" Lucas said.

"Oh," the three-year-old said, after a deep and serious pause. "Did somebody *have* an accident?"

"Nobody had an accident."

"Did somebody get dead?"

"Nobody got dead."

"But—what does 'dead' mean?"

"It doesn't mean anything," Lucas promised. "There's no such thing in the world. Nobody dies, and nobody forgets, and nobody goes away for a long time, ever," Lucas said.

The three-year-old weighed the issue with immense concentration for a moment through the darkness. "That's *great,*" he said at last, and dropped with a sigh back to sleep.

———◇———

A few hours later Lucas awakened earlier than anyone in the world: earlier than the three-year-old, certainly, who was lying half off his bed like a knight who'd been jostled from his horse by another knight; earlier than Wanda and the baby, who lay together in one bed in the other room like lovers in a fairy tale, the moment of enchantment at hand. Lucas had been dreaming of shoes—hundreds of shoes of every description and not one of them paired, hundreds of single shoes tap-dancing away from him in every direction possible—and he stepped into the pair that lay openmouthed beside the bed. Outside, the Saturday-morning sky was very bright, brighter than the air it was made of, and windy. Looking up through the window as he dressed in last night's jacket with the crumpled crocus still on it, Lucas saw the clouds bending past the top of the Statler, bending past and tearing apart like wet tissue; looking down, he saw the funny pages of a newspaper chasing each other on the sidewalks like little painted dogs. He was down there, himself, in no time . . . gliding the family station wagon out of the parking lot across the street, traveling slowly up Delaware Avenue in second gear. The empty city reeked of shoe polish. Five blocks along—still in second gear—he saw the first shoes from his dream: incredibly heavy shoes worn by teenagers hunched under sleeping bags, waiting for concert tickets to go on sale. These were shoes made for space-walking, Lucas thought; they were meant to counteract the teenagers' lack of gravity. Still in second gear a few blocks farther, he saw two pairs of old ladies' shoes, shapeless black wax formations worn by two old ladies waiting at a bus stop; they looked like something a large insect might deposit, to keep the ladies *there*. He passed a shoe store, its windows filled with ballet shoes, and silver shoes, and what looked like magical glass slippers out of a fairy tale . . . truly out of an early-morning fairy tale . . . and he drove on until he found Mr. Deerfelt's apartment building. He slowed to a stop against the curb, leaving the engine alive, and in two minutes, as he *knew* would happen, a pure-featured young woman stepped gracefully forth. She was wearing light-brown shoes of an unfashionable suede material that made her feet appear mousy; just the sort of shoes Lucas would expect to be on sale behind the Iron Curtain. They were the shoes of a young woman who did not care about pretty shoes, or about trendy things at all; who trusted, rather shyly, that her beauty would come through despite whatever she wore—it would come through in her music, and in her voice. It was the trust these shoes expressed, the wary innocence, the sense of sorrow and idealism, that Lucas sensed at once—knew immediately—could be none other than the trust and wary innocence and sorrow and idealism of a violinist who'd been brought over in the last year from Warsaw; and Lucas wanted to talk to her for a minute, for only a minute, for a short-enough time so that he could be back in the hotel room before any of his family even knew he'd been gone . . . about nothing, about something silly and yet important—about escargots: how delicious they tasted, how achingly mouth-watering, to someone who hadn't had them in years and years.

"Veronica!" he cried out. "Veronica! Veronica!"

The graceful young woman in the light-brown shoes looked over her shoulder at Lucas and smiled. "Sorry," she said. "Wrong girl."